EXCLUSIVE! Tall, dark an̶d̶ ̶...
Ricardo Salvatore has prove̶... ̶...g̶...
spending millions as he is at making them—
and it's all on a new woman...

She's London-based party planner Carly Carlisle. And the pretty blonde has been on his arm at parties in St Tropez, the Hamptons and a chi-chi French Château. At every event they flew in on his private jet or his chopper—and stayed in exclusive private and luxurious villas near the party venues, no expense spared. Ricardo even splashed out nearly £10,000 in St Tropez on designer frocks for Carly Carlisle, fuelling rumours that the rather shy (and allegedly virginal) Carly is now almost certainly his mistress.

All the society snipers are speculating that Carly is just another bimbo after his cash. After all, the St Tropez shopping expedition was simply because Carly 'lost her suitcase'—and they think that's the oldest trick in the book. But my sources confirm that Carly Carlisle is actually very generous. And there is no mistaking the sheer lust between these two— we're talking hot, hot, hot! And I say lucky you, Carly—Ricardo is a legend between the sheets...

BEDDING HIS VIRGIN MISTRESS

BY
PENNY JORDAN

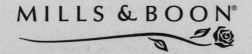

First published in Great Britain 2005
Harlequin Mills & Boon Limited,
Eton House, 18-24 Paradise Road, Richmond, Surrey TW9 1SR

© Penny Jordan 2005

ISBN 0 263 84168 5

Set in Times Roman 10½ on 12 pt.
01-0805-49114

Printed and bound in Spain
by Litografía Rosés, S.A., Barcelona

CHAPTER ONE

CARLY glanced discreetly at the small mixed party she was minding in her role as partner in one of the country's most prestigious and exclusive event-organising businesses, and wondered how long it would be before she could leave. The event was a fortieth birthday party for a banker and he'd chosen to have it at *the* London Nightclub CoralPink. It would not have been the venue she would have chosen but in a business where ultimately the customer was always right that was not her decision to make.

Already, though, she could see that their client's wife was beginning to look less than pleased at the amount of attention her husband was giving the upmarket eye candy on view. There were already half a dozen empty bottles of Cristal champagne on their table, and another of the men was chatting up a girl who had been walking past, inviting her to join them. Male libidos and wifely tempers were both beginning to rise ominously in the club's hormone-drenched heat, Carly realised dispiritedly.

She had balked at this assignment all along, knowing it wasn't her cup of tea. She preferred the kind of event she had supervised over the weekend—a jolly surprise eightieth birthday party held for a sharp-witted grandmother by her large family. It had taken some delicate finessing of finances on Carly's part to ensure that everything they had wanted was achievable within their modest budget, and she had been justifiably proud of the end result.

Mike Lucas's wife was going to explode in a minute if he didn't stop flirting with the young girl he had grabbed. Carly swiftly got up and made her way towards him, intent on defusing the situation before it got out of hand.

Ricardo didn't know why the hell he had allowed himself to be persuaded to come here. His appetite for the proposed business deal that had brought him here had already soured. The whole set-up was everything he loathed, and could best be summed up as rich, immoral men being pursued by greedy, amoral women, he decided cynically.

His attention was caught by the occupants of a table several feet away. A group of forty-something men, paunchy and sweating from a combination of the club's heat and the effect of the skimpily dressed young women thronging the room. Their wives and partners might be younger than they, but they were nowhere near as young as the girls the men were watching—apart from one. She was younger than the rest but still a woman and not a girl, and as Ricardo watched her she got up from her seat and walked round to the other side the table, where one of the men had started to paw a giggling leggy brunette for whom he had just ordered a bottle of champagne.

'Mike.' Carly smiled as she leaned towards him, strategically placing herself between him and the unknown girl.

'Hello, sexy. Want some champagne?'

Mike Lucas made a grab for her, pulling her down onto his knee and putting his hand on her breast.

Immediately Carly froze, warning anger zig-zagging

through the glance she gave him, but Mike was too drunk to notice. Still grinning, he pulled the other girl towards him as well. Unlike Carly, she made it plain that she was enjoying the attention.

'Look what I've got,' Mike called out to his friends, one hand on Carly's breast and the other on the other girl's. He jiggled them inexpertly and boasted drunkenly, 'Hey, what about this for a threesome, guys?'

Ricardo's hooded gaze monitored the small unsavoury scene. The sight of women selling their bodies was nothing new to him. He had grown up in the slums of Naples, and these women—these spoiled, pampered, lazy society women, with their designer clothes and their Cartier jewellery—were, as far as he was concerned, far more to be despised than the prostitutes of the Naples alleys.

He pushed back his chair and stood up, throwing a pile of banknotes down onto the table. The man who had invited him to the club was talking to someone at the bar, but Ricardo did not bother to go over and take any formal leave of him before quitting the club.

As a billionaire he had no need to observe the niceties that governed the behaviour of other, less wealthy men.

Ricardo studied the newspapers the most senior of his quartet of male PAs had left on his desk for him. He read them as he drank the second of his ritual two cups of thick, strong black coffee. Some tastes could be acquired, but others could never totally be destroyed or denied. He frowned, a look that was a formidable blend of anger and pride forking like lightning in the almost basalt darkness of his eyes.

He was not a prettily handsome man, but he was a man who commanded and indeed demanded the visual attention of others—especially women, who were aware immediately of the aura of raw, challenging male sexuality he exuded.

He reached for the first newspaper, flicking dismissively and contemptuously through its pages until he found what he wanted. A smile, in reality no more than cynically bared white teeth against the warmth of the skin tone that proclaimed his Italian heritage, curled his mouth without reaching his eyes as he glanced swiftly down the newspaper's much trumpeted, newly revised 'Rich List'.

He didn't have to look very far to find his own name. Indeed he could count on the fingers of one hand the names that came above his.

Ricardo Salvatore, billionaire. Estimated fortune… Ricardo gave a short, grim laugh as he looked at a figure that fell well short of his actual wealth.

Beneath his name there were also a couple of lines describing him truthfully as single and thirty-two years old, and untruthfully as having founded his fortune on an inheritance from his uncle. A further line offered the information that, in recognition of his charitable donations to a variety of good causes, it was rumoured that Ricardo Salvatore was to be given a knighthood.

Now Ricardo did smile.

A knighthood! Not a bad achievement for someone who had been orphaned by the deaths of his young Italian mother and British father in a rail accident, and who, because of that, had ended up growing up virtually alone in the worst of Naples' slums. It had been a tough and sometimes brutal way to grow up, but occasionally Ricardo felt that he had more respect and admiration for the companions of his youth than he did for the people he now mixed with.

Family ties and close friendships were not things that had ever formed a part of the fabric of his life, but he did not feel their absence. In fact, he actively liked his solitariness, and his corresponding freedom from other people's demands. He had learned young how to survive—by listening and observing—and how to make his own rules for the way he lived his life. He drew his strength from what existed within him rather than what other people thought of him. He had been just eighteen, fiercely competitive and ambitious, when he had gambled for and won the money that had enabled him to buy his first container ship.

He dropped the newspaper onto his desk, picked up the file adjacent to it marked 'Potential Acquisitions' and started to speed-read through its contents. Ricardo was always on the look out for promising new acquisitions to add to his portfolio, and Prêt a Party would fit into it very neatly.

The first time he had heard of the organisation had been when a business acquaintance had mentioned it in passing, commenting that he was a family friend of its young owner. In fact, knowing Marcus Canning as he did, he was rather surprised that a man as financially astute as Marcus hadn't seen the potential of the business for himself.

He gave a small shrug. Marcus's reasons for not acting on the potential of Prêt a Party were of relatively little interest to him. By nature Ricardo was a hunter, and, like all hunters, he enjoyed the adrenalin-boosting thrill of the chase almost as much as he enjoyed the ultimate and inevitable kill at the end of it.

Prêt a Party might only represent a small 'kill,' but Ricardo's preparations for the chase would still be carefully planned.

The normal avenue of obtaining detailed industry reports was not one he favoured; for one thing it tended to alert every other hunter to his interest, and for another he preferred his own methods and his own instincts.

The first thing he wanted to do was find out a good deal more about how the business worked—how efficient it was, how profitable it was, and how vulnerable to a takeover that would be profitable to him. The best person to tell him that was, of course, the owner, Lucy Blayne, but she was hardly likely to equip a potential and predatory buyer with such information. Which was why he had decided to pose as a potential client. The kind of fussy client who wanted to know every single in and out of how things worked and how his commission would be handled before he gave it. The kind of client who insisted on seeing Prêt a Party's organisational capabilities at first hand.

Of course in order to have these 'eccentricities' catered for, he in turn would have to dangle a very large and very juicy carrot in front of Lucy Blayne.

And that was exactly what he was going to do.

'Carly! Thank God you're back! It's absolute chaos here!'

Walking into Prêt a Party's smart but chaotic office in Sloane Street, one of the most upmarket areas of London, Carly acknowledged ruefully that things must indeed be chaotic for her once schoolfriend and now employer—kind-hearted and sweet-natured Lucy Blayne—to be in too much of a rush to ask Carly how things had gone last night.

One pretty but terrified-looking young girl who was new was rushing around trying to cope with the non-stop ringing of the telephone, whilst a couple more, who weren't new, were earnestly reassuring clients that, yes, everything was in hand for their big event.

'We're just sooo amazingly busy—that launch party we did for you-know-who, the It Girl of the moment's new jewellery range, got a mensh in *Vogue*. Nick's bringing us in so much new business,' Lucy enthused.

Carly said nothing. She had done her best not to let Lucy see how much she disliked Nick, and of course there was no way she could tell her friend why. Lucy was deeply in love with her new husband, and Carly knew how much it would hurt her to learn that Nick had actually come on to Carly herself within days of Lucy introducing him into the business.

'Oh!' The pretty young girl looked shocked and almost dropped the telephone receiver.

'It's the Duke of Ryle,' she told Lucy theatrically, in a cut-glass upper-class English voice. 'And he wants to speak to you.'

Lucy rolled her eyes. 'Don't disappear, there's something important I need to discuss with you,' she told Carly quickly, before saying cheerfully, 'Uncle Charles— how lovely. How is Aunt Jane?'

Smiling reassuringly at the flustered and flushed-faced young girl, Carly edged her way past the overflowing desks in the outer office and into her small private office, exhaling in relief as she stepped into her own circle of peace.

A note on her desk caught her eye and she grinned as she read it.

BEWARE—Lucy is in major panic mode—Jules

The three of them—Lucy, Julia and Carly—herself, had been at school together, and Carly knew that Jules, like her, had been extremely dubious at first when Lucy had told them she intended to set up an event organisation company.

But Lucy could be very persuasive when she wanted to be, and since—as Jules had pointed out—neither of them had any other job to go to, and Lucy, thanks to her large trust fund, could afford to both set up the business and pay them a respectable salary, they simply could not refuse.

Now, three years later and much to her own astonishment, Carly had been forced to admit that Lucy's business was beginning to look as though it had the potential to become a really big success. Just so long as she continued to insist that they kept a firm grip both on reality and their costings.

'Come back!'

'Jules!'

'So, how did last night go?'

Carly grimaced expressively. 'Well, let's just say that the tabloid journalist who snapped Mike Lucas with one hand down the front of the Honourable Seraphina Ordley's Matthew Williamson frock and the other gripping my far less worthy, five-year-old second-hand Armani silk-clad breast will by now have realised his mistake. ''Thou shalt not photograph the niece of one's rag's major shareholder in a pose more suited to a failed contestant from *Big Brother*''.'

'Ordley?' Jules mused. 'So she's a Harlowe, then.' As she was an earl's granddaughter, Julia knew *Burke's Peerage* inside out. 'It has been said that the Harlowes' motto should be ''As in name, so in action''. It's a Charles II title,' Jules explained. 'He handed them out like sweets to his cast-off mistresses. You aren't smiling,' she accused Carly.

'Neither would you be if you had been there last night.'

'Oh. As bad as that, was it?'

When Carly made no verbal response, but instead simply looked at her, Jules grinned. 'Okay, okay, I apologise. I should have been the one to go with them, I know, and I backed out and left you to do it for me... Did he really grab your boob, Carly? What did you do?'

'I reminded myself that the evening was making us a profit of £6,000.'

'Ah.'

'And then I dropped a full bottle of Cristal on his balls.'

'Oh!'

'It wasn't funny, Jules,' she protested, when her friend started to laugh. 'I love Lucy to bits and most of the time I'm grateful to her for including me in her plans—like when she decided to set up this business. But when it comes to events like last night's...'

'It was one of Nick's, wasn't it?'

'Yes,' Carly agreed tersely.

'And the weekend—did you manage to get time to see...them?'

Carly frowned. The three of them were so close that there were no secrets between them, but even so the habit of loyalty was ingrained deeply within her.

Jules—or the Honourable Julia Fellowes, to give her her correct title—touched her gently on the arm, and Carly shook away her own reticence.

'It was dreadful,' she told her simply. 'Even now I don't think they've really taken it in. I felt so so sorry for them. They've lost so much—the estate and everything that went with it—and the prestige living there gave them was very important to them. And now this.'

'Well, at least thanks to you they've got a roof over their heads.'

'The Dower House.' Carly pulled a face. 'They hate living there.'

'What? When I think of how you've beggared yourself to get a mortgage and buy it from the estate for them—oh, honestly, Carly.'

'I might not be able to afford a designer lifestyle, but I've hardly beggared myself. Thanks to you I'm living rent-free in one of the poshest parts of London. I've got a job I love, all the travel I could possibly want...'

She had balked initially at Jules's generous offer that the three of them should share her flat—the three of them being Jules, Carly, and Jules's notorious 'I'm having a bad day and I need to shop' habit. Other people ate chocolate, or rowed with their mother; Jules bought shoes.

But who was she to mock other people's security blanket habits? Ever since she could remember she had saved: pennies, and then her allowance...comfort money. Not that it was bringing her much comfort now. Thanks to the needs of her adopted parents, her bank account was permanently empty.

'...and a weight round your neck that no one should have,' she heard Jules telling her protectively.

Ignoring her comment, Carly said, 'I wish I could have stayed for a bit longer. I felt guilty leaving them.'

'*You* felt guilty? That's crazy. Carly, you don't owe them anything. When I think of what they did to you!'

'You mean like giving me a first-class education?' Carly offered her quietly.

It was at times like this that she recognised the huge gap that existed between herself and the other two.

Despite their shared education, they had been born worlds apart.

'You've had to pay for it,' Julia told her protectively.

Carly made no response. After all it was true—but not in the way that Julia had meant. The payment she found unbearable was the knowledge that she was destined always to be an outsider, someone who did not quite fit in—anywhere.

Julia gave her another hug.

Pretty, brunette Julia, and gentle, tender-hearted blonde Lucy—Carly had envied them both, just as she had envied all the other girls at school: girls who knew beyond any kind of doubt that they were taking their rightful place in their own world. Unlike her. She had known she had no right to be there in that alien, wealthy environment. Everything about her had screamed out that she did not and could not fit in. She had felt so out of place—a fraud, a pauper, a charity case, someone whose life had been bought! And, of course, very quickly everyone had known just why she had come to be there.

'Sometimes I wonder what on earth I'm doing in this business.' Lucy exhaled as she came to join them.

'Only sometimes?' Carly teased her.

Lucy grinned.

'We've got a major client scenario about to take place. Nick is on his way over with him right now.'

Carly looked away discreetly as she saw a small shadow touch Julia's eyes. It had been Julia who had introduced Nick to Lucy, and sometimes Carly wondered if Nick, with his flashy pseudo-charm which she found so unappealing, hadn't perhaps made Julia as vulnerable to him as Lucy had been. Was she being overly cynical in worrying that Nick had married Lucy more for her trust fund and her family's social position and wealth than because he had genuinely fallen in love with her? For Lucy's sake she hoped it was the latter, but it had all happened so quickly—too quickly, Carly felt. And now here was Nick, a man she didn't like or trust, taking a very prominent role in the business.

'How major?' Carly asked.

'Jules, call over one of the girls, will you?' Lucy begged. 'I'm dying for an espresso! Absolutely huge. Apparently he knows Marcus—and you can imagine how I feel about that!'

Marcus Canning was Lucy's *bête noir*: a family friend who was also one of her trustees and who, against Lucy's wishes, had insisted on being kept fully informed of every aspect of the business before he would agree to Lucy investing her trust fund money in it. Personally, Carly thought that Marcus Canning, with his well-known reputation for astute financial dealings, was a good person for them to have on board, and she had felt both proud and pleased when he had praised her at their last financial meeting for the way she was running the administrative and financial side of the business.

'And, of course, if he does commission us then we're going to make a bomb!' she heard Lucy announcing enthusiastically.

'Who is he, and what does he want?' Julia chimed in.

'He's Ricardo Salvatore. He's mega-wealthy, and his story is real rags to riches stuff. There was an article in one of the Sunday supplements about him a couple of months ago. He grew up in Naples and he was orphaned very young. But he ran away from the orphanage when he was ten years old and ran wild with a group of children who existed by stealing and begging, generally blagging a living. He's a billionaire now, and he owns—amongst other things—three top-of-the-market exclusive luxury cruise liners. What he wants is for us to organise private parties and that kind of thing for people on these cruises at several villa venues throughout the world. He also owns the villas—and in one case the island it's on.

'He rang earlier, at a very bad moment. In fact, while we were still in bed at home.' She pulled a face and then giggled. 'Poor Nick was…well… Anyway, Nick's just phoned to warn me that they're on their way over here. Ricardo's told him that before he makes a decision he wants to observe a variety of our already planned events, as a sort of unofficial extra guest.'

'What? You're going to let him gatecrash other people's parties?' Carly demanded, shocked. 'Are you sure that's wise?'

'I can't imagine many of our clients would refuse to have a billionaire as an extra guest!' Lucy told her defensively. 'Anyway, Nick has already told him it's okay, and the thing is, Carly, it makes sense if you are the one to accompany him.'

'Me?'

'One of us has to go with him,' Lucy pointed out. 'And besides…' She bit her lip. 'Look, don't take this the wrong way, but I think you'd have more in common with him than either of us, and he'll feel more comfortable with you…'

It took Carly several seconds to catch on, and when she did she her face burned.

'I see.' She knew her voice was tense and edgy but she couldn't help herself. 'So what you're saying is that he's a self-made man, not out of the top drawer and not—'

'Oh, rats. I knew you'd take it the wrong way.' Lucy groaned. 'Yes, he *is* a self-made man, Carly—and a billionaire self-made man at that—but that wasn't what I meant! It isn't anything to do with class! I want *you* to escort and accompany him because I know you'll make a better impression on him than anyone else. Apparently he likes all that stuff you like—reading, museums, galleries. And it is desperately important that we do make a good him impression on him and secure his business.' She paused, and then told them both, 'I didn't want to tell you about this, but the truth is that things haven't being going as well as they were. We had that warehouse fire earlier in the year, which destroyed loads of our stuff…'

'But we were insured!' Carly protested.

Lucy shook her head.

'No, we weren't. Nick felt that the quotes you'd got were too high, and he asked me to hold off paying the premium until he'd checked out some other insurers,' she told her unhappily. 'I thought Nick had gone ahead and insured us with new insurers, but I'd got it wrong, and of course, unfortunately, the existing insurance lapsed.'

Carly frowned. Lucy looked and sounded strained and uncomfortable. She couldn't help wondering if Lucy was trying to protect Nick by taking the blame for his negligence.

She ought to be grateful to this as yet unknown potential client for giving her the opportunity to escape—if only for a while—from her growing discomfort about the way Nick was using the business's bank account as though it were his own private account. Since Lucy had made it clear that Nick was to have *carte blanche* to withdraw money from the account whenever he liked, there was no legitimate objection she could make. Nick had shrugged aside her concern about their growing overdraft by telling her that the deficit would be made good from Lucy's trust fund, but to Carly it seemed shockingly unbusinesslike to waste money paying interest on an overdraft.

'They'll be here in a few minutes. God, I hope we get his business.' Lucy yawned. 'I am sooo tired—and we've got dinner with the folks tonight. How about you? Have you got anything on?'

'Only my writing class,' Carly answered.

'I don't know why you're still going to that,' Julia told her ruefully.

Originally they had decided to attend the writing group together, at Julia's suggestion—mainly, Carly suspected, because Julia had been dating an up-and-coming literary novelist. But after a couple of weeks the romance had faded, and Julia had taken a period of extended leave to visit her sister in Australia, leaving Carly to attend the weekly meetings on her own.

'Mmm…'

'Well, it won't hurt to miss one class, surely? Unless, of course, it's Miss Pope's turn to read one of her poems?' Julia giggled.

Carly tried and failed to give her a quelling look.

'They are pretty awful,' she agreed, joining in her laughter.

'What project has the Professor given you all to write about this time?' Julia gave a small shudder. 'It's not litter again, is it?'

'No,' Carly confirmed carefully, 'it isn't litter. Actually it's fantasy sex!'

It was amazing what the word *sex* could do, she reflected ruefully as both her friends turned to stare at her.

'Fantasy sex?' Lucy demanded. 'What, you mean like…imagining sex with a fantasy man?' She started to laugh. 'Why?'

'Professor Elseworth wants us to stretch our imagination and take it into a new dimension.'

'Right now, any kind of sex is a fantasy for me,' Julia remarked gloomily, before adding, 'But I can't imagine *you* writing about fantasy sex, Carly. I mean, you don't actually do it at all, do you?'

Carly bared her teeth in a ferociously fake smile.

'No, I don't. And I won't until I find someone worth doing it with!'

'Well, okay—I mean, I don't have a problem with that—but how on earth are you going to write about fantasy sex when…?'

Carly gave her a withering look.

'I'm going to use my imagination. That is the whole point of the exercise,' she told her with awesome dignity.

'Rather you than me!'

'No talking about sex during working hours,' Lucy began mock primly, and then stopped as, to Carly's relief, their newest recruit arrived with Lucy's espresso.

In all honesty she would be only too happy to have an excuse to miss out on her writing class and its assignment. She certainly didn't want to write about fantasy sex—or indeed sex of any kind. She knew there was a barrier between her and the potential enjoyment of her sexuality. But how could she ever give herself freely and openly, to a man and to love, when she could never imagine being able to reveal her emotional scars to him? How could there be true intimacy when she herself was so afraid of it? So afraid of being judged and then rejected? Didn't events such as the one she had attended last night confirm all that she had always thought and feared? Giving yourself in and with love to another human being meant giving yourself over to being judged as not good enough, not acceptable, not worthy, and ultimately to rejection. And she had learned very young just how much that hurt.

Her game plan for her life involved focusing on emotional and financial security: building her career, enjoying the company of her friends, ultimately travelling—if she could afford to do so—but always ensuring that she never made the mistake of falling in love.

She had decided that she was only going to have a sexual relationship if she met a man she wanted physically with intense passion and hunger—a man with whom she knew she could share the heights of physical pleasure in a relationship that carried no health risks. A serial male sexual predator was not an option. And at the same time she would also have to feel one hundred per cent confident that she would never be at risk of becoming emotionally involved with him. Add to that the fact that she wasn't even actively looking for this paragon, and it seemed a pretty foregone conclusion that she was likely to remain a virgin indefinitely.

Not that the prospect bothered her.

CHAPTER TWO

'AND you're sure my requirements won't be a problem for you, Nick? I know you don't have a large staff,' Ricardo said blandly.

'Absolutely not. Lucy said that Carly jumped at the chance. In fact she begged for it.' Nick laughed. 'And I don't suppose anyone can blame her. After all, when you've been used to the best of everything all your life and suddenly it isn't available any more, and you're a decent-looking woman, I suppose you're bound to look forward to spending time with a rich man.'

'She's looking for a rich husband?'

Nick grinned.

'Who said anything about marriage? Anyway, come up to the office and I can introduce you to her.'

'I think you said earlier that she is your wife's partner?'

'Employee. The three of them—Lucy, Julia and Carly—were at school together. Neither Julia nor Carly have put any money into the business, though.'

'So financially the partnership is—'

'Just me and Lucy,' Nick informed him.

'Carly normally does all the financial and administrative stuff, but to be honest I don't think she's up to the job. You'd be doing me a favour by taking her off my hands for a week or two, so that I can get the financial side of things sorted out properly. Lucy's a loyal little soul, and devoted to her friends—you know the type, all breeding and no brains.' He shrugged. 'I don't

want to say too much to her. Anyway, having Carly
with you won't be too much of a hardship—she's a
good-looker, and obliging too, if you know what I
mean—especially if you treat her generously. Like I
said, Carly has her head screwed on.'

'Are you speaking from personal experience?'
Ricardo asked him dryly.

'What? Hell, no. I'm a married man. But let's just
say she let me know that it was available if I wanted
it,' Nick boasted.

He was well aware that Carly didn't like him, and it
amused him to think of what he was setting her up for.
Discrediting her wouldn't do him any harm in other
ways either, he congratulated himself. For one thing she
wouldn't be able to go tittle-tattling to Lucy.

'Carly is very good at getting other people to pay her
bills for her—as both Lucy and Julia already know.
She's even managed to blag a rent-free room in Julia's
flat. If she can't find a rich man to finance her, then the
lifestyle that working for Prêt a Party gives her is the
next best thing. All that first-class travel and accom-
modation provided by the clients, plus getting to mingle
with their guests.' He winked at Ricardo. 'Ideal for her
type of woman. Once I've introduced you, I'll get her
to go through the list of our upcoming events with you
so that you can cherry pick the ones you want to attend.'

'Excellent.' Inwardly, Ricardo decided that Nick
sounded more like a pimp than a businessman. Or in
this business did the two go hand in hand?

They had reached Prêt a Party's office, and Nick
pushed open the door for him.

'Ah, there's Carly,' he announced. 'I'll call her over.'

There was no way she could pretend not to be aware
of Nick's summons, Carly had to acknowledge reluc-

tantly, and she walked towards him. She was wearing her normal office uniform of jeans and a tee shirt—the jeans snugly encased the slender length of her legs but irritatingly, the tee shirt skimming the curves of her breasts had pulled free of the low waistband of her jeans. It was a familiar hazard when one was almost five foot ten tall, give or take one eighth of an inch, and it exposed the flat golden flesh of her taut stomach. Whenever she could, Carly ran—mostly on her own, but sometimes with a group of fellow amateur runners—and her body had a sensuous grace of which she herself was totally unaware.

Long thick hair, honey-brown, with natural highlights, swung past her shoulders as she walked calmly towards Nick—and then missed a step as she saw the man standing to one side of him.

If she were in the market for a man—sex-wise, that was, because she would not want one for any other reason—then this was definitely a man she would want. She could feel the power of his sexuality from here; she could breathe it in almost. And it was very heady stuff. Far more potent than any champagne, she thought dizzily.

A vulnerable woman—which, of course, she was not—would find it almost impossible to resist such a man. He was a living, breathing lure for the whole female sex. Except for her. She had exempted herself from such dangers.

Ricardo frowned in immediate recognition as he watched her walking towards them and coldly came to two very separate decisions.

The first was that he intended to have her in his bed, and the second was that she embodied everything he most disliked about her class and type.

She was stunningly beautiful and irritatingly confident. And he already knew from listening to Nick that
she was a woman who judged a man by his wallet and
how much she could extract from it. A gold-digger, in
other words.

'Hello, gorgeous. Let me introduce you to Ricardo—
oh, and by the way, Mike Lucas rang me to tell me how
much he enjoyed your company last night,' Nick told
Carly, as he put his arm round her shoulders and drew
her close to his side.

Pulling herself free, Carly extended her hand to
Ricardo and smiled at him with genuine pleasure. After
all, he was going to be releasing her from the unpleas-
antness of Nick's unwanted company.

Well, she certainly didn't believe in wasting any
time, Ricardo thought cynically as he took the hand
Carly had extended and shook it firmly.

'Ricardo wants to have a look at our upcoming events
so that he can decide which ones he wants to attend.
You can use my office, Carly,' Nick told her benignly.

His office? Carly had to look away. 'His office', as
he called it had, until he had come onto the scene, been
her office. In fact it still was her office, she reflected,
since she was the only one who did any work in it.
Nick's only appearances in it were when he came in to
ask her to countersign another cheque.

Carly smiled as she led the way to the small sec-
tioned-off cubicle where she worked. Ricardo had lost
count of the number of women who had smiled at him
the way Carly was doing right now—with warmth and
promise—especially women of Carly's type. Upmarket,
privately educated pampered women, contemptuous of
the very idea of supporting themselves, whose goal in

life was to find a man to financially underwrite their desired lifestyle.

His gaze narrowed. Female predators were a familiar risk to any man to whom the press attached the label 'wealthy'; he had discovered that a long time ago. He had been twenty-two and merely a millionaire the first time he had encountered the type of well-bred young woman who believed that a man like him—a self-made man who had come up from nothing—would be delighted to spend lavishly on her in exchange for the social cachet of being connected with her.

She had been the sister of the thrusting young entrepreneur with whom he'd had business dealings. Initially he had thought he must be mistaken, and that she couldn't possibly be coming on to him as openly as she'd seemed to be. He had indeed been naïve. There had been an expensive lunch to which she had invited herself, he remembered, and an even more expensive afternoon's shopping, when she had pointed out to him the Rolex watch she wanted. Like a besotted fool he had gone back to the shop and bought it for her the moment she had left him to return to her brother. He had then, even more besottedly, booked himself out of his hotel room and into a huge suite, had ordered a magnum of champagne and the most luxurious meal he could think of, and then wasted more time than he cared to think about dreaming of the pleasure that lay in store for them both. He would make love to her as she had never been made love to her before, and then, in the morning, he would kiss her awake and surprise her with the watch…

He had very quickly been brought back to earth when, instead of relishing his tender caresses, the object of his adoration had told him peevishly to 'hurry up', and then pouted and sulked until he produced her watch. The final blow to his pride, though, had been unwittingly delivered by her brother, who had informed him that his sister was as good as engaged to an extremely wealthy older man. Fortunately, although his illusions had been shattered, his heart had been left intact, and the whole experience had taught him what he considered to be a valuable lesson: the only difference between spoilt, pampered society women and the prostitutes of Naples was that the prostitutes had no option other than to sell themselves if they wanted to feed their children.

He had yet to meet a woman whose desire for him did not go hand in hand with her desire for his money, no matter how much she might initially deny it. Indeed, if he hadn't been so fastidious he knew that he would have found it cheaper to hire the services of a professional than to satisfy the financial demands of the society women who had shared his bed. The discovery that the last one to do so had been contemplating being unfaithful to him with an elderly billionaire old enough to be her grandfather had confirmed his cynical belief that no woman was too beautiful or too well born to be above using her 'assets' to secure financial security.

He would take Carly to bed and he would ensure that both of them enjoyed the experience, and that would be that. Why shouldn't he take advantage of what she was? She was a beautiful woman, and it was a very long time since he had last had sex, but her social standing cut no ice with him, and nor was he impressed by it—quite the opposite, in fact.

'Here's a list of our upcoming events and their venues,' Carly announced a little breathlessly, after she had printed it off from the computer.

She hadn't expected to be so acutely aware of Ricardo's powerful and sensually invasive sexual aura. She wasn't used to this kind of man, and there was an unfamiliar flutter in her stomach and a hyped-up sensation of excitement in her head. She felt both excited and apprehensive, as though somehow her whole body had moved up into a higher gear, a more intense state of awareness. It was simply her hormones responding to his hormones, she told herself prosaically. Her office was way too small for the two of them.

Out of the corner of her eye she saw that he was removing his suit jacket, and she discovered that she was sucking in an unsteady breath of reluctant female appreciation. Beneath the fine cotton of his shirt she could see the muscular hardness of his body. She had recently read an article in a magazine about the new fashion for men to wax their chest hair. He obviously didn't subscribe to it.

The author of the article had propounded the theory that women found the abrasion of male body hair unwelcome against their own flesh. Carly's tongue-tip touched her lips. A fine mist of sensual heat had broken out on her skin. Beneath her tee shirt her bra-covered breasts suddenly ached, her nipples pushing against the restraining fabric.

How could she be having such intensely sexual thoughts about a man she had only just met? It must be because she had been talking about sex to Lucy and Jules. Yes, that was it; her mind was obviously more focused on sex than usual.

He was still studying the list she had given him, plainly oblivious to what she was experiencing, and of course she was glad about that—wasn't she? After all, she had never been the kind of woman who felt piqued because a man didn't show any interest in her.

Because until now she had not met the right kind of man?

'Perhaps if you were to tell me what kind of event you are thinking of having I might be able to pick out the best events for you to attend,' she suggested hastily.

'I haven't made up my mind as yet.'

Carly looked blankly at him. She had naturally assumed that, like their existing clients, he must have a specific event in mind.

Ricardo permitted himself a small cynical smile. If his plans went ahead as he expected, the first event Prêt a Party would be organising for him would be a party to celebrate his acquisition. But of course he wasn't going to tell Carly that. She, he had already decided, would be one of the first surplus-to-requirements 'assets' of the business to be offloaded.

'I understand you are responsible for the administration and accounts of the business?'

'Er, yes...'

'You must be very well organised if you can carry out those duties and still have time to accompany clients to their events.'

'I don't normally. That is, I stand in for the others sometimes.'

She was making it sound as though she had to be coerced into doing so, Ricardo thought cynically. Of course he knew better.

'Carly, your mother's telephoned. She wants you to ring her—Oh, I'm sorry.' The young girl who had burst into the office came to an abrupt halt, her face pink, as she realised that Carly wasn't on her own.

'It's all right, Izzie, I'll ring her later. Thank you.'

But as she thanked the younger girl Carly's heart was sinking beneath her professional smile. She already knew what her adoptive mother would want. More money.

Carly did her best, but the truth was that the woman had no real understanding of how to manage money. The fortune her adoptive father had once had was gone, swallowed up in lavish living and unwise investments. A stroke had made it impossible for him to do any kind of work, and so Carly found herself in the position of having to support them as best she could. But it wasn't easy. Her adoptive mother ran up bills and then wept because she couldn't pay them—like a small child rather than an adult. Their anguished unhappiness and despair made her feel so guilty—especially when...

She was so lucky to have friends like Lucy and Jules, Carly reflected emotionally. She might get on reasonably well with her adopted parents now, but that had not always been the case. Without Lucy and Jules what might she have done to escape from the misery and the wretchedness that had been her own childhood? Taken her own life? She had certainly thought about it.

Where had she gone? Ricardo wondered curiously, watching anxiety momentarily shadow her eyes before she blinked it away. He cleared his throat.

'Right. Here are the events I wish to attend.'

Pushing back her private thoughts, Carly leaned over the desk to study the list he had tossed towards her.

He had selected three events: a private party in St Tropez on board a newly acquired private yacht, to celebrate its acquisition; a media event in the Hamptons to launch a new glossy magazine, to which old money, new names and anyone who was anyone in the fashion world had been invited and a world-famous senior rock star's birthday bash at his French château.

Carly started to frown.

'What's wrong?'

'The St Tropez yacht party is next weekend, and only four days before the Hamptons do. It might be difficult co-ordinating flights and all the other travel arrangements.'

She kept a tight rein on expenses—or at least she had done until Nick had started to interfere. They always booked cheap, no frills flights to overseas events if they weren't being flown out by the clients.

Ricardo raised an eyebrow.

'That won't be a problem. We'll be using my private jet.' He gave a dismissive shrug of those powerful shoulders. 'One of my PAs can sort out all the details. Oh, and they'll need your passport, ASAP. I understand from Nick that your normal practice is to be *in situ* a day ahead of the actual event. That suits me, because that way I shall be able to see how things are organised.'

Too right he would, Ricardo decided.

He was standing up, and Carly followed suit. He was so tall—so big! She was suddenly aware of her reluctance to go through the doorway, because it would bring her too close to him. Too close to him? Get a grip, she mentally advised herself unsympathetically.

'My PA will be in touch with you regarding flight times.'

She walked determinedly towards the door. She was almost level with him now. In another few seconds she would be through the door and safe. Safe? From what? Him pouncing on her? No way would he do that, she told herself scornfully.

And then she made the mistake of looking up at him.

It was like stepping through a door into a previously unknown world.

Her heart whipped round inside her chest like a spinning barrel. Against her will her head turned, her lips parting as her gaze fastened on his mouth. His top lip was well shaped and firmly cut, his teeth white and just slightly uneven, and his bottom lip…

His bottom lip. A smoky sensuality darkened her normally crystal-clear grey eyes as she fed visually on the promise of its fullness. How would it feel to catch that fullness between her own lips? To nibble at it with small biting kisses, to…

'A word of warning—' Ricardo began.

She could feel guilty colour staining her skin as her mind grappled with inexplicable thoughts.

'It is imperative that full confidentiality as to the purpose of my attendance at these occasions is maintained at all times.'

He was cautioning her about the events—that was all! Carly exhaled in shaky relief.

'Yes—yes, of course,' she agreed quickly, as she finally made it through the doorway on legs that had developed a very suspicious weakness.

But she was unnervingly aware of him behind her.

'And one more thing.'

'Yes?' she offered politely, automatically turning round to face him.

'The next time you look at my mouth like that…' he said softly, with a mocking smile.

'Like what? I didn't look at it like anything!' Carly knew that her face was burning with guilt, but she had to defend herself.

'Liar. You looked at it, at *me*, as though you couldn't wait to feel it against your own. As though there was nothing you wanted more than for me to push you up against that doorframe and take you right here and now. As though you could already feel my hands on your skin, touching you intimately, and you were loving it. As though—'

'No!' Carly denied fiercely. And her denial was the truth—she hadn't got as far as thinking anything so intimate as that!

To her relief she could see Lucy hurrying towards them to introduce herself to him.

It was over an hour since Ricardo had gone, and Carly was still thinking about him. But a woman would surely have to be totally devoid of any kind of hormones to remain unaware of Ricardo as a fully functioning man.

And that was her sole excuse, was it? She pushed back her keyboard and stood up. She was shaking slightly. Her face was burning and her body ached. She felt shocked. Guilty. Horrified, in fact, by the door she had unwittingly opened in her own head, and—even worse—was uncomfortably aware that she was physically aroused. Physically, but of course not emotionally—that was impossible. After all, she had sworn never to fall in love, hadn't she? Never to fall in love; never to give herself emotionally to anyone; never to risk the emotional security she had given to herself.

She started to pace the small office. Her childhood had taught her all there was to know about the pain that came with being emotionally rejected. She had fought hard to give herself the protective air of calm self-confidence she projected to others, and for the right to claim their respect. The pathetic, needy child she had once been, desperate for approval and love, had been totally banished, and that was the way Carly intended it to stay.

So why was she thinking like this? No one was threatening her self-reliance, after all—least of all Ricardo Salvatore, who probably had the same loathing of emotional bondage as she did herself, if for very different reasons.

CHAPTER THREE

CARLY checked her watch—Lucy had given both Carly and Jules smart Cartier Tank Francaise watches for Christmas in the first year the business had made a profit—and then bent down and grabbed the handle of her case.

The car Ricardo Salvatore was sending to pick her up was due to arrive in exactly two minutes' time. It was time for her to leave.

She heaved her suitcase off the floor, grimacing a little ruefully as she did so, remembering how Lucy had burst into the office the previous Thursday morning announcing, 'Oh, my God, Carly—I've just realised! There won't be anything in the Wardrobe that will fit you!'

The 'Wardrobe' was a standing joke between them all, and was in actual fact a small room in Lucy's parents' London home which housed the glamorous outfits Lucy and Jules, who were very much the same height and build, wore when they were 'on duty' at events.

The clothes—all designer models—were second hand, surreptitiously trawled from a variety of sources, and the subject of amused speculation between them.

'Just look at this!' Lucy had marvelled after their last expedition, as she held up what looked like a sequin-covered handkerchief with halter neck straps. 'Who on earth would buy this?'

'You did,' Carly had pointed out, laughing.

'Yes, but *I* only paid fifty pounds for it—it cost over a thousand brand-new.'

'It's very sexy,' Jules had pronounced.

'It's repulsive,' Carly had criticised. 'Vulgar and tarty.'

'Mmm… Well, Nick spotted it.'

But the Wardrobe contained nothing that would fit Carly, and so, that Thursday, Lucy had announced firmly, 'Come on, Carly. We've got to go out on a trawl!'

Carly had tried to protest and resist, but Jules and Lucy had been insistent.

The result of their foray into the second-hand shops and market stalls of Lucy's favourite haunts—which had emptied the clothes budget Carly had so carefully worked out—had been collected from the dry cleaners this morning and were now packed in Carly's case, along with her own clothes.

Mentally Carly reviewed them—a white silk trouser suit which Lucy had cooed over, enraptured, pronouncing, 'Oh, this is so retro—Seventies rock wife! And you've got the boobs for it, Carly.'

Maybe she had, but she certainly wouldn't be wearing the jacket over bare skin and half open! There were also a couple of evening dresses, both of which were potentially so revealing that Carly had already decided she would be wearing a silk jacket over them.

She hadn't been very keen on the designer swimsuit Lucy had found either. It was cut away in so many places that Carly feared it threatened to reveal more of her than the skimpiest of bikinis, but at least it had matching culotte pants and a jacket.

Her own classic casuals—the simple linen separates she favoured for summer and some up-to-the-minute ac-

cessories they had found in the likes of Zara—had all
passed Lucy's inspection and been declared perfect for
the events she would be attending.

Dragging her suitcase behind her, Carly pushed open
the door onto the street and stepped out into the late-
morning sunshine.

Ricardo watched her from his vantage point in the
back seat of the limo, as the driver moved the car out
of the parking bay he had found further up the street.

Oh, yes, she was a typical example of her upmarket,
'no expense spared but someone else pays' lifestyle,
Ricardo decided cynically as he watched her. Immaculate white tee shirt, perfectly fitting blue jeans, long
shiny hair, minimal make-up, sunglasses, discreetly
'good' watch, penny loafers. The too-thin girl in designer clutter who was tottering past her on spindly
heels, clutching a weird-looking handbag, couldn't hold
a candle to her. Because Carly had *class*.

What would she be like in bed?

He didn't intend to let too much time elapse before
he found out.

He thought of another society woman from his youth,
one whom he had met when he was growing cynical
but not yet completely hardened. Initially he had
thought her pretty, but she hadn't looked very pretty at
all when he had flatly refused to meet her escalating
demands—especially when he'd discovered they included a wedding ring in exchange for the supposed
benefit of marrying into a higher social bracket. He'd
told her that he preferred an honest whore.

Women like her, like Carly, might not openly demand money in return for sex, but what they were looking for was the richest and highest status man they
could find—their bodies in exchange for his name.

It was a trade-off that nauseated him, as did those who participated in it.

He had no illusions about women or sex. He had lived too long and seen too much for that. His wealth could buy him any woman he wanted, and that included Carly. She had made *that* plain enough already, with the way she had looked at his mouth.

She hadn't even tried to be subtle about it! She had stared openly and brazenly at him. If they hadn't been in her office it would have been an open invitation to him to push her tee shirt out of the way and free her breasts to spill into his hands so that he could accept their flaunting invitation.

It had told him that he could have yanked down her jeans and explored and enjoyed her and she would not have said a single word in denial.

And then in the morning she would no doubt expect to receive her payment—a piece of jewellery, a telephone call from an exclusive shop inviting her to choose herself something expensive...

That was the way things were done in her world.

He was wasting too much time on her, he warned himself. His primary reason for what he was doing was the potential acquisition of Prêt a Party, not the inevitable sexual acquisition of Carly Carlisle who, although she did not know it yet, would be one of the first in line to lose her job.

Carly frowned as the large, elegant steel-grey car drew up alongside her.

A limo, Lucy had said, and she had pictured a huge, shiny black ostentatious vehicle, not something so supremely understated. But the rear door was opening and Ricardo was getting out.

'Is this all your luggage?'

She gaped at him as he reached for her case, and then looked uncertainly towards the chauffeur.

'Charles is driving. I am perfectly capable of picking up a case,' Ricardo told her dryly, following her uncertain look.

'The…my case is heavy,' she told him, but he ignored her, picked it up and put it in to the boot of the car as if it was as light as a feather pillow.

He was wearing a black tee shirt and a pair of tan-coloured casual trousers, and the muscles in his arms were hardening as he lifted her case. He looked more like a man who worked outdoors than one who sat at a desk, she acknowledged, unwilling to admit to the response that the sight of him was eliciting from her own body.

After what had happened when she had given her imagination its head, she was now keeping it on a controlling diet of bread and water, and that meant no thinking about the effect Ricardo could have on her! So he had a good enough body to carry off the macho male thing—so what? she told herself dispassionately.

But the sight of his black-clad back, bent over the open boot, suddenly transformed by her rebellious thoughts into a totally naked back bent over her equally naked body, evoked such a powerful sensual image that she felt as though she were transfixed to the spot.

So it was true. You *could* go weak at the knees, Carly reflected several minutes later as she sat primly straight in the back seat of the powerful car, dizzily aware that her private thoughts were anything but prim. All those enforced deportment classes at school had definitely left her with an automatic 'sit up straight' reflex.

She was accomplished, Ricardo admitted to himself. That cool, remote pose she had adopted, that said *Pur-*

sue me would certainly work with most men. Unfortunately for her, he was not most men. He opened his briefcase and extracted some papers.

As soon as they were free of the city traffic the powerful car picked up speed. Carly was pleased that Ricardo was engrossed in his work, because that left her free to think about hers, instead of having to make polite conversation with him.

Since their clients were using their own yacht as the venue for their party there was no construction work in the shape of marquees on the like for her to oversee. The client's chef and kitchen staff were being augmented by a chef from the upmarket caterers she had sourced. They were already on the yacht. Menus had been agreed, floral arrangements decided on—she would be meeting with the florists, who had also been flown in from London.

The arrival and deployment of the hostess's hairdresser, make-up artist, and a dresser from the couture house she favoured were also Carly's responsibility, plus a hundred or more other small but vitally important arrangements.

She had an inch-thick pile of assorted coloured and coded lists in her briefcase, most of which she had actually memorised.

'You're so much better at this than me,' Lucy had told her ruefully before she left.

Carly had smiled, but she knew that it was true.

Carly shifted her body against the leather upholstery. It was ridiculous that she should be so acutely conscious of Ricardo's presence in the car with her—and even more ridiculous that she should be so acutely aware of the impact he was having on her physically. So much for the 'bread and water' regime, then!

The grand slam of his raw sensuality had sliced through her defences, leaving an alarming trail of female awareness in its wake. Her jeans, normally a comfortable easy fit, suddenly seemed to be uncomfortably tight, clinging to her flesh in a way she could only mentally describe as erotic, as though somehow she were being caressed by the lean, powerful male hands she couldn't resist looking towards.

She could feel the heat expanding inside her, dangerous little languorous curls of it thrusting against her sensitive flesh. She crossed her legs and then uncrossed them. Her arm accidentally brushed against her own breast and immediately she was aware of the hot pulsing of her nipples.

This was *crazy*. It felt as though somehow or other an unfamiliar and certainly unwanted very sexual alter ego had been released inside her. And, what was more, it seemed to be attempting to take her over! Or had it always been there and it had simply taken meeting Ricardo Salvatore to make her aware of it, just as her own senses were making her aware of him?

This was definitely crazy.

She realised with relief that they had reached the airport. The car slowed down and turned into an entrance marked 'Strictly Private'.

A uniformed customs officer stepped out of a nearby office and came over to the car.

'Your passport, please,' Ricardo demanded, turning to Carly.

Foolishly, she had not been ready for this formality, and it took her several seconds to open her bag, find her passport, and then hand it over to Ricardo.

As he took it from her, her open bag slipped from her hand, showering the immaculate leather and the car's floor with coins, her lipstick, her purse and several other small personal items.

Her face hot, she undid her seatbelt and tried to pick them up as fast as she could, but the lipstick rolled away out of her reach with the movement of the car as the driver set it in motion again.

To her dismay the lipstick had rolled along the leather and come to rest right next to Ricardo's thigh.

She couldn't retrieve it without touching him.

She moistened her lips with the tip of her tongue.

'Could I have my lipstick, please? It's… You're sitting on it,' she told Ricardo.

'What?'

The look he gave her was totally male and uncomprehending.

'My lipstick!' Carly repeated. 'It fell out of my bag and now it's…'

She looked meaningfully at the leather seat, somehow managing at the same time to keep her gaze off his thigh.

His sigh was definitely exasperated as he reached down and picked up the small slim tube.

It was a relief to release her own pent-up breath as he handed the lipstick to her. She reached out for it, too focused on what she was doing to be aware of a deep pothole in the tarmac, which the driver couldn't avoid because of an oncoming vehicle.

The violent movement of the car flung her bodily against Ricardo, sending her slamming into his side. The air was driven out of her lungs by the force of the impact, leaving her half lying against him, her face buried in his tee shirt, her hand ignominiously clutching at his arm.

A shock of unfamiliar sensation hit her all at once, like a hail of sharp-pointed arrows. His personal man-scent, the texture of his tee shirt, the hardness of his chest beneath her cheek, the softness of something that she realised must be his body hair. The slow, heavy thud of his heartbeat...

Somewhere inside her head unwanted images were forming. A man—Ricardo—carrying her in his arms, his torso bare, his flesh warm beneath her fingertips. She could feel the heat of her own desire for him. Her fingers tightened automatically on his arm, her nails digging into his flesh.

Abruptly Carly snapped back to reality, and to the humiliating awareness of what she was doing. Her face burning, she released Ricardo's arm and pulled away for him, refusing to look at him.

As she retreated to her side of the car Ricardo shifted his own position and turned away from her, to conceal the telltale thick ridge of flesh pressing against the fabric of his trousers.

He was beginning to realise that he had badly underestimated the effect Carly was going to have on him. It was one thing for him to acknowledge to himself that he was happy to have sex with her, but it was quite another to have to admit that his desire for her was far more urgent than he had planned for—and, even worse, that it was threatening to overwhelm his self-control. He simply did not want this fierce, thrusting surge of need, this urgent, compelling hunger to take hold of her and fill himself with the scent and the feel of her; the taste of her, to fill her *with* himself and to...

The ache in his body was intensifying instead of fading, and he had to resort to the subterfuge of opening his newspaper and busying himself re-reading it in order to conceal that fact.

*   *   *

'Thank you, Charles.'

Carly had no time to do more than smile her own gratitude at Ricardo's chauffeur before a smartly uniformed flight steward was escorting her up the steps to the waiting private jet, whilst Ricardo paused to speak with its captain—*his* captain, Carly realised.

She had often heard Lucy marvelling about the luxury of travelling in the private jets owned by some of their more wealthy clients, but this would be the first time she had experienced it for herself.

The interior of the jet had more resemblance to a modern apartment than to any aeroplane Carly had flown in. A colour scheme of off-white and cool grey set off the black leather upholstery of the sofas, and the steward discreetly indicated to her that both a bedroom and a separate shower room lay to the rear of the sitting area.

'The galley is behind the cockpit, and there is another lavatory there as well—' He broke off from his explanations, to say formally, 'Good morning, sir.'

Carly turned round to see Ricardo standing in the open doorway.

'Morning, Eddie. How are Sally and the new baby?'

There was a genuine warmth in his voice that touched a painful nerve within Carly's heart.

'They're both fine. Sally was over the moon that you flew her folks here for the birth. She was resigned to them not being able to be there.'

Ricardo shrugged, and changed the subject. 'Phil says that we're going to have a good flight, both to Nice and on to New York.' He turned to Carly. 'I've got some work I need to attend to, but feel free to ask Eddie for anything you need.'

'If you would like to sit down here, madam, until we've taken off?' Eddie suggested politely to her, indicating a space on one of the sofas.

Obediently, Carly went and sat down.

'Perhaps I could get you a glass of champagne?' the steward said, once he had shown Carly how to use her seatbelt, and explained to her how to access the power and telephone lines for her laptop should she wish to use it. 'We've got a very nice Cristal.'

Carly couldn't help it. She gave a small shudder. 'Water will be fine,' she told him emphatically.

From his own seat at a desk on the other side of the cabin, Ricardo frowned. Why had she refused champagne? She certainly hadn't been having any qualms about drinking it the night he had seen her in CoralPink.

Thanking Eddie for her water, Carly unzipped her own laptop. Ricardo wasn't the only one who had work to do. Five minutes later, as the jet taxied down the runway, Carly was deeply engrossed in reading her e-mails—but not so deeply that she wasn't acutely aware of Ricardo's presence.

She couldn't forget the disturbing effect those fleeting seconds of physical intimacy in the car had had on her. Her stomach muscles clenched immediately, as though in rejection of the response she had felt, her mouth going dry.

Eddie had said the jet had a fully equipped bedroom... The ache inside her sharpened and tightened and then started to spread.

The jet lifted off the tarmac and Carly held her breath, willing herself not to think about Ricardo.

'I'd like to ask you a few questions about certain aspects of the way Prêt a Party's business works.'

Dutifully Carly put aside the list she was studying. Ricardo was, after all, a potential client.

'Were I to commission Prêt a Party to organise an event for me, who would be responsible for establishing the cost of everything involved?'

'I would,' Carly answered him promptly.

'And would you do that by sourcing suppliers yourself? Or does someone else—Lucy, for instance—source suppliers?'

'Normally I would source them. We've been in business for long enough now to have established a core of suppliers we use on a regular basis. However, sometimes a client will specify that they want to use a specific caterer, or florist, or musician. When that happens we either negotiate with them on the client's behalf or, if the client prefers, they negotiate with them themselves. If they opt to do that then we ask that the clients also make themselves responsible for paying the supplier's bill. When we're in charge of suppliers' estimates and invoices we know exactly what their charges will be—that isn't always the case if the client has commissioned a supplier.'

'Presumably you obtain good discounts from your regular suppliers?'

'Of course, and we pass them on to our clients via our costings for their events. But discount isn't the main criteria we apply when selecting suppliers. Quality, reliability, exclusivity are often more important to our clients than cut-price deals.'

'What do you do when potential suppliers offer to make it worth your while to select them?'

Carly couldn't look at him, and she could feel her face starting to burn. Since Nick had joined the business she had received several such approaches from suppliers, who had insisted that Nick had promised them work. Nick himself had tried to pressure her into using them, but Carly had refused to do so. She knew that Lucy would never have authorised such dishonest business practices, but she hadn't felt able to tell her friend what her husband was doing because she didn't want to hurt her. And she certainly couldn't tell Ricardo—a potential client—about them.

'We…I…I make it plain to them that that we don't take bribes and that they are wasting their time,' she hedged, uncomfortably aware that she was not being totally honest.

Ricardo looked at her, but she was refusing to look back at him, her body language reflecting both her guilt and the lie she had just told him.

Backhanders from suppliers would add a very sizeable 'bonus' to Carly's salary, Ricardo thought grimly.

It surprised him that she wasn't making more use of the fact that they were alone and in the intimate surroundings of the jet in order to let him know that she was available. And did that disappoint him? He shrugged the thought aside. Hardly. He had simply assumed that she would want to showcase her skills for his benefit.

He recognised the discreet little come-ons that women like her were so adept at giving, such as leaning close to him whilst pretending to show him something, so that he could breathe in her perfume—which he had not as yet been able to identify other than to be aware that it suited her. A good quality signature perfume? Custom blended? Expensive! Blended exclusively for her? *Very* expensive! By one of the top three perfumiers? Very expensive—and paid for by a very rich and very doting man!

At least she had not had a boob job. He had been aware of that the moment she'd fallen against him. But she was wearing a bra, a plain, seamless, no-nonsense tee shirt bra. Unusual for a woman out to snare a man, surely? And unnecessary, in view of the excellence of the shape and firmness Mother Nature had generously given her.

Had she leaned over him now, he would have lifted his hand to caress her breast and even, had he felt so inclined, pushed aside her tee shirt and bra and explored the shape and texture of her naked breast, both with his fingers and his lips.

He found himself wondering idly if her grooming regime went as far as a Brazilian wax. He personally wasn't enamoured of the look, although he knew of men who insisted not just on a Brazilian but that their lovers go for the full Hollywood 'everything-off' wax. He personally preferred something a bit more natural, a bit more sensual. And she had such thick, luxuriant, clean and shiny hair—the kind that made him want to reach out and touch it. He moved uncomfortably as he tried to change the direction of his thoughts.

'We'll be landing in a few minutes.'

Carly smiled at the steward and put away her papers. She would be rather glad to get off the plane, although not because she was afraid of flying—at least not in the non-sexual sense. There she was again! Thinking about sex.

And all because… Because what? Because secretly she wanted to have sex with Ricardo? Chance would be a fine thing, she mocked herself. But if she were to be given the chance…

The first thing Carly noticed as they came out of the airport was the small group of beggars—children, not adults—clustered pathetically together whilst people ignored them. Thin and dirty, wearing shabby torn clothes, they stood out amongst the seething mass of people to-ing and fro-ing, and yet everyone was acting as though they simply did not exist. The smallest of them was barely old enough to walk.

Ricardo had gone to collect his valet parked rental car, telling her to wait where she was.

She had noticed a sandwich shop on her way out of the airport, and now, impetuously, she came to a swift decision. Wasn't the golden rule to give food rather than money because money might be taken from them? Dragging her case behind her, she hurried back to the sandwich bar.

The children watched her approach without interest. Their pinched faces and emotionally dead eyes wrenched at her heart. When she handed them the food, small claw-like hands snatched it from her.

'Euros,' the older children demanded sullenly, but she shook her head.

She could see people looking disapprovingly at her, no doubt thinking she was encouraging them to beg.

Her mobile was ringing. Carly felt a familiar sense of anxiety and despair twist her stomach when she saw that the caller was her adoptive mother—she could never think of her as anything other than that, and she was, she knew, bound to her adoptive parents by guilt and duty rather than love. Guilt because she did not love them, and because she was alive whilst their own flesh and blood daughter was dead.

Fenella had made her life a misery when they were growing up together, and her death from a drugs overdose had not been the shock to her that it had been to her parents—how could it, in view of the number of times Fenella had turned up at her flat either to beg or harangue her into giving her money to fund her habit? And of course when they were growing up Fenella had been the loved and valued one, whilst she… Automatically she clamped down on her thoughts. She was an adult now, not a child.

It took her several minutes to find out what was wrong. Her adoptive parents had run up a bill of several thousand pounds for which they were past the stage of final demands and warnings and which they could not now repay. How could they have spent so much? Carly felt slightly sick. She did some mental arithmetic and heaved a small sigh of relief. She had just about enough in her own accounts to cover it.

'Don't worry—I'll sort everything out,' she promised, fighting not to feel upset at the thought of such a large sum of money—to her—being wasted. Ending the call, she turned towards her case, her eyes widening as she stared in disbelief at the empty space where it should have been.

Carly was trying desperately not to give in to her panic as she saw Ricardo striding imperiously towards her.

'The car's this way.'

Somehow or other he had relieved her of both her laptop and her hand luggage.

'Where's your case?'

Her mouth went dry with panic.

'I…er… It's gone,' she told him uncomfortably, well aware that she probably only had herself to blame, and that her act of charity had badly backfired on her.

'Gone?'

'Yes. I think someone must have stolen it.'

Ricardo absorbed her none too subtle message cynically. Managing to 'lose' her luggage was certainly a dramatic start to setting him up to replenish her wardrobe. What *had* she done with it? Put it in a left luggage locker?

'So now you don't have any clothes to wear?' he offered helpfully. He would play along with her for now, if only to see her *modus operandi* in action.

Carly exhaled shakily, relieved that he was taking it so well.

'No—nothing apart from what I'm wearing.' And, thanks to that desperate phone call she had just received, she wouldn't be able to afford to replace what she had lost either, she realised with growing dismay.

'Annoying, I know. But at least you'll be able to claim on your insurance policy later,' he told her dispassionately, and then watched her. He had to admit that she was very good—that small indrawn breath, that tiny betraying flicker of her eyelashes, which demanded a response. 'You are insured, I trust?'

'I do have insurance,' Carly agreed.

But it was not the kind of insurance that would enable her to replace her carefully chosen designer wardrobe, she realised dispiritedly.

'So there isn't any problem, is there?' Ricardo offered smoothly. 'After all, you are in one of the best places in the world for female retail therapy, aren't you?'

'I'm sure it's certainly one of the most expensive,' Carly agreed wryly.

'I'd better find a police station and report it, I suppose.'

Ricardo listened appreciatively. She was *very* good.

'I doubt that would do any good. You can report it by phone later from the villa, if you wish.'

He was impatient to leave and she was holding him up, Carly realised at his crisp words. And he was a potential client.

So what did she do now? She couldn't keep her promise to her adoptive parents, to whom she needed to transfer the money quickly, *and* replenish her wardrobe. None of her small 'for her old age' investments could be realised quickly, and she was loath to put a further charge on the business by asking Lucy for money to replace clothes *she* was responsible for losing—especially since they had emptied the budget and cash flow was problematic.

This was not a good time to remember the lecture she had delivered to both Jules and Lucy about how they should follow her example and refuse to possess any credit cards.

She had a few hundred euros in cash—petty cash and personal spending money—probably about enough to buy herself some new knickers, she acknowledged derisively.

Which meant…

What? It was a Saturday; her bank would be closed. Attempting to arrange a temporary bank loan here, with her limited French? Not a good idea. Ringing Jules, explaining what had happened and asking her for a temporary loan? Better—if Jules was even there. But Jules would probably tell Lucy, and then Lucy would insist on sending her money from the business. Asking someone else if they could help her out? Like who? One of their contractors? Or… She looked uncertainly at Ricardo as she followed him to the car.

There was nothing she hated more than being beholden to someone, accepting a benefit she could neither repay nor return. It went against everything she believed in to ask anyone to even lend her money—and were the money for her own personal spending she would have starved rather than consider it. But it wasn't. It would just be temporary. And she had a duty to the business that surely overrode her own pride?

As they reached the car Ricardo looked at Carly. It was obvious to him that she was expecting him to do the gentlemanly thing and offer to replace her lost clothing. Poor girl—how on earth could she be expected to manage with just the contents of her hand luggage and the clothes she stood up in? She couldn't—and, since effectively she was here at least in part for his benefit, naturally he, as a very wealthy man should offer to provide her with a suitable new wardrobe.

And when he didn't respond as she obviously wanted him to, what, he mused, would be her next move?

Did St Tropez have second-hand clothes shops? Charity shops? Carly wondered worriedly as she thanked Ricardo when he politely held open the passenger door of the car for her. Surely it must. French women were known to be shrewd in such matters.

'Something wrong?' Ricardo asked her smoothly.

She was very tempted to admit just how much was wrong—although she doubted he would share her dismay at the thought of a £4,000 bill, she thought ruefully. She opted for discretion instead, and told him lightly, 'I didn't realise you'd be driving yourself. I was expecting a chauffeur-driven car.'

Of course she was. Women like her did.

'Even billionaires sometimes like to economise,' he told her dryly, before adding, more truthfully, 'I like driving, and I grew up in Naples. If you can drive there and live, you can drive anywhere.'

The car was plain and solidly built, but—blissfully—the air-conditioning was wonderfully effective.

They were stationary in a queue of traffic, and at the side of the road a young man was offering a stunningly pretty girl a peach. As Carly looked on, the girl, oblivious to everything and everyone other than the young man, leaned forward and cupped her hand round his. Then, without taking her gaze from his, she took a bite out of the ripe fruit whilst its juice ran from it onto their interlocked hands.

The small tableau was so intensely sensual and intimate that Carly immediately looked away—and found she was looking right into Ricardo's eyes.

Could he see in hers that she had watched the young couple, wondering how it would feel if *he* had been the one offering the peach to her? If its juice had run on *her* bare skin, would he have bent his head to savour its path with his tongue? Would he have...?

She started to tremble violently, small beads of sweat breaking out on her skin, and her body was suddenly thrown forward against her seatbelt as Ricardo depressed the accelerator savagely, causing the car to shoot forward.

What the hell was the matter with him? Ricardo berated himself silently. No way was he dumb enough to fall for something so obvious as the tired old come-on Carly had just tried out on him. *Look at my lips, watch my tongue, imagine...*

It was those damned eyes of hers that did it! How the hell did she manage to get them to turn so smoky and lustrous with desire on demand like that?

Hell—insanely, for a second, she'd almost had him

persuaded that the sight of those two kids with their peach had made her ache for him as if he was the only man on earth. Not that his body needed much persuading. It was all too eager to believe she wanted him.

CHAPTER FOUR

'WHERE exactly are we staying?' Carly asked Ricardo, hoping that it would be within easy walking distance of the town and the harbour. She would need easy access to both from early tomorrow morning, so that she could liaise properly with their contractors and get to the bank, as she had promised her parents, plus somehow find time to replenish her wardrobe.

'Villa Mimosa,' Ricardo answered her. 'It's outside St Tropez itself, up in the hills overlooking the sea. I'm not a particular fan of over-hyped, supposedly *in* places. Invariably, every minor celebrity that TV and magazines have ever created flock to them for maximum publicity exposure, destroying whatever charm the place may once have had. I like my privacy, and personally I prefer quality to quantity every time.'

'Oh, yes. Me too,' Carly agreed immediately. 'But I do need to be able to get into St Tropez quickly and easily.'

'Ah, you're thinking about replacing your missing clothes,' Ricardo said affably.

Carly couldn't help laughing. 'That, yes—but I was thinking more of liaising with our contractors.'

'Mmm. I thought the purpose of this trip was for you to liaise with me,' Ricardo told her softly.

Damn and double damn. He cursed himself mentally as he saw Carly absorbing the subtle flirtatiousness of his remark. Why the hell had he done that? Why hadn't he waited and let her come on to him? Now she knew he was receptive to her!

Ricardo had just flirted with her! A heady mixture of pleasure and excitement danced along her veins. Careful, she warned herself. Remember you don't want to get into a situation you can't afford. On the other hand, there was such a thing as being too cautious. After all, her common sense told her that a man like Ricardo would not be interested in anything more than the very briefest kind of relationship—a 'no commitment of any kind' type of relationship. The perfect kind of relationship, surely, for a woman like her, who did not want to fall in love but who secretly—even if this was the first time she had admitted it to herself—wondered what it would be like to have sex with a man all her instincts told her would be a once-in-a-lifetime lover. Why shouldn't she live a little recklessly for once?

'Well, I certainly want to do my best to please you.'

Carly could scarcely believe such words had come from her own lips. Words that, no matter how demurely she had spoken them, could surely only convey to Ricardo a very provocative message.

Ricardo turned his head to look at her. That was more like it!

The look in those dark eyes was quite unmistakable, Carly recognised, as her heart missed a beat and sweet, hot, sensual arousal poured through her body like warm honey.

'We're here.'

'What? Oh. Yes.'

She had actually blushed, Ricardo marvelled as he stopped the car. And her nipples were standing out beneath the fabric of her tee shirt in flagrant sexual arousal.

Ridiculously, suddenly he was as hot for her as though he were a mere youth and this was his first time.

She might as well ask for his help and get it out of the way now, Carly decided. Because once they got inside…

Once they got inside *what*? Once they got inside she hoped he would take her to bed?

Her thoughts were leaving her torn between shock and delight. And urgency! Suddenly she wanted very much to get the matter of her need for a short-term loan and her discomfort about mentioning it to him out of the way.

So that she could be free to encourage him to flirt with her and ultimately—maybe—take her to bed without it hanging over her?

The unfamiliar recklessness of her own thoughts took some getting used to. But she wasn't tempted to abandon them, was she?

So first things first, and then…

She cleared her throat and took a deep breath.

'Ricardo… I…er…'

The husky little catch in her voice was very effective, Ricardo thought, as he waited for her to continue.

'I feel very uncomfortable about this, but…'

'Yes?' he encouraged when she pretended to falter. After all, he reasoned cynically, the sooner he could get this farce over with, the sooner he could satisfy the itch to possess her that had now become an almighty, savage, unignorable ache.

Carly took heart from the kindness in Ricardo's patient encouragement.

'I need to replace some of the things that were in my suitcase. I don't want to worry Lucy—it's my job to deal with the accounts, after all—and… And I know this is…' Her face had started to burn. 'I was wondering if I could ask you to lend me some money—just temporarily, of course.'

Why had she ever thought this was a good idea? Carly wondered, feeling acutely embarrassed. Just listening to herself as she stumbled over her words made her go cold with horror at what she was doing. And if *she* found her request unacceptable, then what on earth must Ricardo be thinking?

'I feel dreadful about this,' she admitted honestly, 'but I can't think of what else I can do.'

Really? Didn't she possess a bank account of her own? A credit card? A debit card? The ability to walk into a bank?

'It would just be a loan. I would pay you back, of course…'

Indeed she would—and with interest.

Several different potential responses presented themselves to him, but in the end he decided that, since Carly was so patently thick-skinned, he might as well go for the oldest and least believable of all of them.

So he smiled at her, and then he took hold of her hand and patted it. And then he told her smoothly, 'I shall be delighted to help you. How much do you think you will need?'

She was gazing at him starry-eyed, her face slightly flushed, her lips slightly parted, as though she could hardly believe her good fortune.

Such a heroic effort deserved a generous reward, Ricardo decided cynically.

'Wait! I've had a better idea.' But she, of course, had no doubt already had the same idea before him. 'Why don't we go into St Tropez together tomorrow and you can choose whatever you think you may need?'

For some reason she didn't look as delighted as Ricardo had expected.

Ricardo had made her a wonderful offer, but she was not sure it was one she felt comfortable with, Carly reflected, as she thanked him.

'That's very generous of you.'

'I'm delighted to be able to help,' Ricardo assured her, before adding, 'Come on, let's go inside.'

Carly was used to staying in beautiful and magnificent properties, but the Villa Mimosa was truly breathtaking. Its setting alone—tucked into a hillside, overlooking the Mediterranean—provided a view that must surely always catch at the heart.

From the balcony of her bedroom she could look out over immaculate gardens and across a miraculous infinity pool to the horizon, and although it was a couple of hours now since they had arrived at the villa she still kept going to the balcony and gazing at the view.

The middle-aged Frenchwoman who had welcomed them had explained that she was the maid but that she did not live in. Cathy must have looked rather surprised at that, she realised, because after she had left them Ricardo had explained to her that he preferred to have his own personal staff on hand or do without.

'My own people know how I like things done, and they know too that I like my privacy. It's mid-afternoon now, and I have some business matters to attend to,' he had told her, 'so why don't we agree to meet up on the terrace at, say, six? My choice would be for us to eat in,' he had added suavely. 'I can arrange to have something delivered.'

Carly had felt her heart miss a couple of beats at the potential implications of dining alone with him.

'That sounds perfect,' she had answered, and then worried when she had seen the gleam in his eyes that she had sounded naïvely over-enthusiastic.

Six o'clock, he had said. And it was five now. She might not have anything to change in to, but she certainly intended to shower and tidy herself up.

Half an hour later, showered and still wearing the thick towelling robe she had found hanging up in the bathroom, she was just brushing her hair when she heard a soft tap on her bedroom door. It opened and Ricardo walked in, carrying two well filled champagne glasses.

'I've mixed you a Bellini. I hope you like them.'

'Oh, yes. Yes, I do,' she agreed.

Unlike her, he was fully dressed, in dark linen trousers and a white linen shirt, his bare brown feet thrust into soft plain leather sandals.

He came over to where she was sitting and put one glass down on the glass-topped dressing table, then held the other out to her.

'Try it first,' he urged her.

Sipping from a glass whilst he held it surely shouldn't be such a sensually intimate experience, should it? And why couldn't she stop looking at the long brown fingers curled round the stem of the glass? She tried to focus on something else, but discovered that the only other thing to focus on was his body, and that the place where the line of his trousers was broken by a telltale bulge was exactly on her eye line. And, what was worse, she couldn't seem to stop herself from gazing appreciatively at it.

'It's lovely,' she assured him hurriedly, taking a sip and then turning away. 'I hadn't realised that was the time. I'd better hurry up and get dressed.'

He gave a small shrug.

'You might as well stay as you are. I hope you like lobster by the way.'

'I love it,' she told him truthfully.

'And I also hope that the gourmet meals-on-wheels outfit who brought the food are as good they are supposed to be. I thought we'd eat outside on the terrace.'

He was obviously expecting her to go with him, Carly realised. A bathrobe wouldn't normally have been her first choice of dinner outfit, but on this occasion it seemed she had no alternative.

'I really am grateful to you for being so kind about the money,' she told him.

'Good. Maybe later you might find a way of showing me how much, mmm?'

Ricardo watched cynically as somehow or other she managed to summon a look of shocked bemusement quickly followed by hot excitement into the smoky darkness of her eyes. But his cynicism wasn't stopping him from wanting her, was it? he reminded himself. In fact he had spent the last three hours thinking about very little other than satisfying that want. Which was why, in the end, he had given in to it and gone to her room.

Was Ricardo saying what she thought he was saying? Carly wondered dizzily. Or was she letting her own erotic imagination run away with her?

At least Lucy and Jules would be pleased to learn she was about to abandon her virgin status. Abandon…it was such an emotive word, such a sensual word. And, recklessly, she was already eager to abandon herself to the physical pleasure of Ricardo's possession.

'Or would you prefer to make a start now?'

Carly's eyes widened as he came to within a few

inches of her and bent his head toward hers, his hand resting lightly on the side of her face.

She had never been kissed like this before. There was no physical contact other than that of their lips and his fingers lightly caressing her face. His mouth moved more fiercely on hers and Carly responded instinctively, moving closer to him, leaning into him as his tongue drove deeper into the soft recesses of her mouth to take possession of it.

She started to raise her arms, wanting to hold him, but to her confusion he stopped her, gripping her shoulders and releasing her mouth to step back from her.

Whilst she looked up at him in confusion he untied the belt of her robe and then pushed it off her shoulders in one swift easy movement that left her totally naked in front of him. Her only covering was the hot wave of colour that beat up under her skin. His gaze dropped to her body with the swift descent of an eagle to its prey. It stalked slowly over creamy slender shoulders, down to ripely rounded breasts, softly heavy with sensual promise, silky pale skin contrasting with the darker aureoles from which her rose nipples thrust so eagerly.

Her ribcage curved into a narrow waist, below which her hips flared out again, and her legs were, as he had already known they would be, unbelievably long and perfectly shaped. A soft cap of downy dark curls formed a neat little triangle just above the delicately shaped outer lips of her sex, curled protectively over it.

A dozen—no, a hundred different sensations and desires struck him, which in the end were only one need, one desire, and that the most ancient and powerful of all male needs and desires.

His gaze was fixed on her as though her body was a visual magnet from which he could not look away.

He wanted her. He wanted her right here and right now. He wanted her as he had never wanted any woman before. His own flesh was so immediately and intensely aroused that it was almost painful.

He wanted to take her quickly, fiercely, hotly plunging his flesh within hers and filling her, as though in taking her he would somehow drive out his own need for her.

And yet at the same time he wanted to savour the experience of having her, to relish it and wait for it.

Carly felt like a…a houri in front of a sultan—aware of her own nakedness before him and in some weird way actually physically excited by the fact that he was seeing her like that. Because she knew that he desired her, and his desire for her gave her power over him? The telltale bulge had now become a definite and openly defined ridge of flesh she badly wanted to reach out to and caress. Carly touched her tongue-tip to her lips.

No man had looked at her in the way Ricardo just had. With such a blazing heat of desire that she could have sworn she'd actually felt its burn against her skin.

But then no man had ever seen her like this—stripped bare, vulnerable, the whole of herself revealed.

She could feel a small, excited pulse beating inside her body.

Ricardo was picking up her Bellini and handing it to her. Uncertainly she took it from him. 'You have a beautiful body,' he told her emotionlessly. 'I'm tempted to tell you to stay like this, so that I can continue to have the pleasure of looking at it, but I'm not sure my self-control could go the distance.'

He bent down to pick up her robe and handed it to her.

When she learned forward to take it from him, he

lowered his head and took one taut nipple into his mouth. Could those fierce pangs she felt deep inside her body really be caused by the fierce tugging of his mouth on her nipple? She heard herself moan and was afraid she might collapse. Her legs felt so weak. And yet when his mouth was no longer there she ached for its return, she realised, as he pulled her robe back on for her as unceremoniously and as swiftly as he had removed it.

'More wine?'

Should she? Carly stared into her empty glass. 'No. No more,' she told him firmly, aware of how quickly what she had already had to drink had gone to her head.

It had been heaven eating out here on the secluded patio. The night air was soft and scented, the smallest of warm breezes was caressing her skin, and the moon was a fat yellow disc up above them.

She gave a small sensual shiver, acknowledging that the memory of those few minutes in her bedroom had left a very erotic imprint on her body.

'More lobster?'

Carly shook her head.

'No?' Ricardo questioned softly. 'You're satisfied, then, in every single way?'

He reached across the table and took hold of her hand, caressing it lightly.

How on earth could Ricardo touching her hand cause her throat to constrict? Carly wondered helplessly as she gazed at him, unable to speak.

She was extremely clever, Ricardo acknowledged. She obviously knew from past experience that men liked to do their own hunting. She had let him know she was available, and now she was sitting back and letting him set the pace.

He released her hand and stood up. Carly looked up uncertainly. Ricardo smiled back at her and held out his hand. A little breathlessly, she pushed back her chair and stood up herself. Holding her hand, he drew her towards the low wall that separated the terrace from the rest of the garden.

'Wait,' Carly protested, just before they reached it.

He watched her as she wriggled swiftly out of the robe. She had been aching to do it all through the meal, unable to stop thinking about how she had felt and how he had looked at her earlier on. She had never previously given any thought to her own nakedness in terms of its erotic appeal, but now she was acutely aware of the warm touch of the night air on her skin, and the gloriously wanton feeling that knowing Ricardo couldn't stop looking at her was giving her.

Ricardo felt as though the air was being ripped out of his lungs, whilst at the same time the darkest kind of male pleasure was exploding inside him.

He took hold of her, imprisoning her between his own body and a thick mass of geraniums tumbling over the wall, his hands at the curve of her waist, his mouth fastening on hers.

Carly melted into him, her lips parting eagerly in invitation, her arms winding round his neck. His tongue, deliberately pointed and hard, thrust against her own, its stabbing movement making her moan and shake with pleasure. She wanted him to give her more of it, to fill the hot, wet cavity he was pleasuring until she could take no more of him.

She whimpered in pleasure and arched her body into his, removing one hand from his neck to unfasten his shirt buttons.

She was just as he had known she would be! Just like

every other woman who had looked at him and seen an easy future for herself, Ricardo told himself. But his hands were still sliding up over her ribcage to mould the warm weight of her breasts; his fingers were seeking the eager hardness of nipples as swollen and firm as small thimbles.

She moaned against his tongue as he played with them, caressing and rubbing them, and her own fingers struggled with his zip before she finally managed to slide it down.

He had expected her immediately to touch him intimately, but instead she moved closer to him, rubbing herself sensuously against him with a soft sound of pleasure.

Her height meant that she fitted him as perfectly as though they had been made for one another. He released her breasts and allowed her to rub their sensitive tips against his flesh, his hands supporting her back and then massaging it, shaping her spine and going lower, to cup the rounded curves of her buttocks, hold the bones of her hips. His hand slipped lower, his fingers finding the cleft between her legs. He might not be able to see the ripe readiness of her desire-swollen lips, but he could feel it. His fingers dipped seductively into the wetness of her sex.

She made a sound deep in her throat and moved eagerly against him, the movement of her body against him in time with the thrust of his tongue within the soft, dark cave of her mouth.

His body was straining against her, and the moment he moved she looked down, her gaze fastening on the swollen, darkly veined head of his sex.

His fingers stroked the length of her wetness, caressing her more intimately with each stroke until she felt hot and open, her eager moans inviting him to plunge deeper. Her fingertips were just skimming the hard outline of his penis, almost as though she was afraid to touch it. Or was she simply enjoying tormenting him because she knew how much he wanted her?

Perhaps he should punish her a little for doing that to him?

Punish her and please himself, he thought hotly, as his fingertip massaged the slick wetness of her clitoris and he felt her whole body jump and then shudder wantonly.

Her fingers were circling him, holding him, exploring him, her touch cool against his own heat.

He had to have her.

Carly made a small mewling sound of pleasure deep in her throat and reached out for him, cupping his face with her hands and pressing her mouth passionately against his. All she wanted—all she would want for the rest of her life—was this, and him.

Abruptly she pulled back from him.

Her heart was thudding unevenly with the shock of her thoughts and feelings. Her emotional thoughts, and her equally emotional feelings. She felt sick and shaky as reaction set in and she recognised her own danger. How had this happened? How had she gone from wanting to have sex with to him to wanting *him*?

'What's wrong?'

She was too engrossed in her own thoughts to hear the sharp warning of male frustration in Ricardo's voice.

'I'm sorry… I…I don't think this is a good idea…'

Ricardo could taste the raw savagery of his own furious disbelief. How could he have been such a fool as to let her play him so cleverly? To let her arouse him to the point where nothing mattered more than him having her?

'So what would make it a good idea?' Ricardo demanded bitingly, gripping her arms and swinging her round so hard that she almost stumbled. 'Or should I say how much would make it a good idea? Five thousand? Ten? *Carte blanche* on a credit card?'

Carly stared at him in bewildered shock.

'And you can cut that out,' Ricardo told her. 'I've known what you are from the start. Nick Blayne made it plain enough—not that he needed to. It was obvious what you were from the night I saw you in that damned club, letting someone else's husband paw you.'

A slow, achingly painful form of semi-numbness was creeping up over her body, paralysing her ability to move.

'Well? Come on—answer me. Obviously the promise of a ''loan'' wasn't enough. So what else are you after? A new designer wardrobe? A Cartier diamond? Nick told me that you were good at recognising how to get the maximum amount of financial benefit out of a relationship.'

Belated anger seared through her. 'I'm certainly good at recognising what he's doing to the business—and ultimately to Lucy,' Carly told him hotly. Humiliation was scorching her skin as she absorbed what Ricardo had said to her—what he had said *about* her.

'Well?' Ricardo demanded again, ignoring her furious outburst. 'How much?'

'Nothing,' Carly told him proudly. 'You could have had me for nothing, Ricardo. For no other reason than that I wanted you, for nothing other than the benefit to me of having sex with you.'

'What?' He gave her a derisively cynical look. 'We

both know that that's a lie, and it's not even a good one. You are the one who called a halt.'

Yes, she had. But not for the reasons he was so insultingly suggesting. And she certainly couldn't tell him now why she had wanted to stop.

'You are so wrong about me. I would never—have never—' She stopped as she saw the contemptuous look in his eyes.

'What about the money you asked me for?'

The money she had wanted to borrow from him? Of course—in his eyes that had damned her.

'You don't understand—that *was* just a loan. I *will* pay you back,' she told him quietly.

Ricardo was in no mood to be placated.

'Oh, I think I do understand. Let's see. You pretend to lose your suitcase, then you come on to me, expecting that I will take the bait. Then when I do you immediately back off, thinking that I'm going to ache so damned much for you I'll do anything to have you. How complicated to understand is that?' His mouth twisted in open contempt.

She had thought she knew what it was like to have her pride ripped from her, leaving her exposed to people's contempt, but she had been wrong, she recognised through the blur of her shocked, anguished, furious humiliation. But what was even worse was that she now knew exactly what he had really been thinking about her.

Automatically she tried to defend herself, protesting emotionally, 'You're wrong!'

But he stopped her immediately, challenging her. 'About what? You coming on to me?' He shook his head. 'I don't think so. Not that you didn't get something out of it yourself, so don't bother trying to pretend you didn't. No woman gets as hot and wet as you did and—'

It was too much. Carly reacted immediately and instinctively, her pride driving her to react in a way that was pure, instinctive, emotionally wounded female.

She raised her hand, but before she could do any more Ricardo was gripping her wrist in a bruisingly painful hold.

'If you want to fight dirty that's fine,' he told her softly. 'But remember I grew up on the streets. If you hit me, then I promise you I shall retaliate in kind.'

When he saw her face he laughed. 'No, I don't hit women. But there are other ways of administering punishment!'

'You are a barbarian!' Carly whispered shakily. 'And you have no right... You are totally wrong!' Tears of reaction were stinging her eyes now, but no way was she going to let him see that. 'I only asked to borrow the money because I didn't want to worry Lucy.'

'Yes, of course. Blame someone else. Women like you are very good at that.'

Carly had had enough. 'You don't know the first thing about a woman like me!'

'On the contrary, I know a very great deal.' Ricardo stopped her sharply. 'I know, for instance, that you are the product of generations of so-called good breeding, that your parents are wealthy and well connected, but that you yourself do not have any independent means. You also went to one of the country's top schools. In short, you believe you have an automatic right to the very best of everything and an even more deeply ingrained belief that because of what you are you are superior to those people who have not had your advantages. You expect to be granted a first-class passage through life, preferably paid for by someone else. You are a taker, a user—a gold-digger.'

Something—a bubble of either pain or hysterical laughter—was tightening her chest and then her throat.

'And I know that *you* are a prejudiced, ill-informed misogynist. And—as I've already said—you know nothing about me,' she told him shakily, before turning on her heel and walking away from him.

Alone in the safety of her room she gave in to the tremors of aftershock racking her body, holding onto the back of a chair to steady herself. One day—maybe—she would look back on this, on *him*, and what he had said to her, with irony and perhaps even amusement. Because he was so breathtakingly, hugely wrong about her.

But for now… For now she would be grateful to him for showing her how easily she could have slipped into the emotional danger she had always feared and for going on to destroy every single tendril of those tentative feelings. At least now she was safe from feeling anything for him other than furious outrage.

Were it possible for her to do so, she would leave the villa immediately. But she had Lucy and the business to think of, and Carly had been taught from a very young age to carry a dual burden of gratitude and responsibility.

She would have to stay, and she would have to remember why she was here and why he was here, and behave towards him with all the professional courtesy she could muster.

For the rest, she would rather go naked than ask him for so much as a rag to cover her—would rather starve than accept a crust from his table, rather die than let him see how very much he had hurt her and in how many different ways.

'I know what you are,' he had said.

But the truth was he did not know her at all.

The truth was… The truth was a secret, and so painful that she could not bear to share it with anyone.

CHAPTER FIVE

CARLY stood on the harbourside, her eyes shaded by dark glasses, as she and the chefs ticked off the items being delivered.

It was eleven o'clock in the morning and she had been up since half past five. Luckily she had managed to persuade a taxi driver to pick her up from the villa, despite the earliness of the hour, initially to go to the flower market with the florist, Jeff, and his team to ensure that the freshest and most perfect blooms were purchased for the party, and then to accompany the two chefs when they bought the fresh produce they needed.

She was trying very hard not to keep looking at the strip of pale flesh where her Cartier watch had been. She had loved it so much—not because of its monetary value but because of what it represented. The owner of the small shop she had found tucked down a narrow alley had expressed neither curiosity nor surprise when she had handed over her watch in return for a wad of euros and a pawn ticket. Once she got home she intended to speak with her bank and arrange to either take out a loan or realise some of her assets so that she could both buy it back and give herself a small cash reserve. She hated the idea of being in debt, but there was nothing else she could do.

As soon as she could snatch an hour she intended to replace the lost clothes as best she could. Which wasn't going to be easy. True, she had seen a wide variety of trendy shops and boutiques on her way to and from the

74

market, but the clothes at the cheaper end of the market were really only suitable for the very young, whilst those she would have considered suitable were way, way out of her price range.

Luckily, on her way back from the flower market she had spotted a stall selling casual holiday wear and had been able to buy a pair of three-quarter capri pants and a couple of tee shirts. Buying new underwear had proved a little more difficult, but eventually she had found the small shop she had been recommended to try, tucked down a side street off Rue Georges, and had been able to buy a pack of plain white briefs and a simple flesh-coloured bra.

Behind them the harbour was filled with the huge white luxury yachts of wealthy visitors, but the yacht belonging to Prêt a Party's client surely had to be the most expensive and glamorous looking of all.

Carly had been given a tour of it earlier by Mariella D'Argent's PA, Sarah, who had also generously offered Carly the use of her own small cabin to change in, and had then insisted on taking her travel-worn clothes to the yacht's laundry, promising that Carly would have them back before evening.

'It's a pity we aren't the same size, otherwise I could have loaned you something,' she had commiserated when Carly had told her what had happened with her luggage. 'Mariella is, though,' she had added thoughtfully. 'Okay, she may be a bit taller...'

'And at least two sizes thinner,' Carly had tacked on, laughing.

Mariella D'Argent, their client, had been one of the fashion world's best known and best paid top models before her marriage to her financier husband, and even now, at close to forty, she was still an exceptionally stunning and beautiful woman. And an even more exceptionally spoiled one, Carly had decided, after listening politely to her fretful demands.

'Mmm, and guess how she stays that way.' Sarah had grimaced. 'I swear to heaven one of these days she's going to get it wrong—sniff Botox up the new nose her surgeon has had to construct for her and inject cocaine into her wrinkles. And then, of course, there's always the danger that she might take his Viagra whilst he takes her Prozac—or at least there would be if they still shared a bed.'

Carly had tried not to laugh.

'Anyway, what about one of those fab silky floaty cotton kaftans that are all the rage? A short one, worn over some slinky cream or white pants, and perhaps a stunning belt—that would look terrific. Or a sarong tied round them, perhaps? That's a very cool look now,' Sarah had suggested helpfully.

Carly had nodded her head and smiled, even whilst knowing that the type of oh, so casual but oh, so expensive items Sarah was referring to were completely outside her budget. She had seen the kaftans Sarah had described on her way down to the harbour this morning. Gorgeous, silky fine floaty wisps of cotton, with wonderful embroidery and a price tag of well over a whole month's salary!

The party was due to start at ten o'clock in the evening, prior to which the D'Argents were holding a 'small' dinner party for fifty of their guests onshore.

'So, what do you think of this?'

Dutifully Carly gave her attention to the clever arrangement of greenery and mirrors the florist had used to create a magical effect, making the small reception area appear far larger than it actually was.

'Very impressive, Jeff,' she told him truthfully.

Their own construction crew were speedily finishing erecting a framework for the tenting fabric, which was cream with a design on it in black to complement Mariella D'Argent's theme for the evening: cream, black and grey.

Currently a redhead, she, of course, would look stunning in any combination of such colours!

Looking at the fabric, Carly thought briefly of persuading the man in charge of the construction crew to give her a piece. Wrapped around plain black trousers it would look stunning—but perhaps just a bit too obvious? On the other hand, wearing it, she should be able to melt into her surroundings!

A rueful, mischievous smile illuminated her face— and that was how Ricardo saw her as he drove into the harbour area.

He had thought at first when he got up that she was still sleeping, and it had been nearly midday when he had finally decided to go and check on her.

The discovery that she had left the villa without him knowing had caused him a quixotic mix of emotions, the most dangerous and unwanted of which had been a shaft of pure male possessiveness and jealousy,

Because she had aroused him? She was far from the first woman to have done that, and he certainly hadn't felt possessive about any of the others!

Deep down inside himself Ricardo was aware of the insistent and powerful effect she had on his emotions. She made him feel incredibly, furiously, savagely angry, for one thing. For another, she was making him spend far too much time thinking about her.

He was still several yards away from her when Carly suddenly became aware of his presence, alerted to it by a sudden tingling physical awareness that had her turning round apprehensively.

Dressed in natural-coloured linen trousers and a white linen shirt, dark glasses shielding his eyes from the brilliant glare of the sun, he looked utterly at home against the moneyed backdrop of St. Tropez, and Carly was not surprised to see several women stop to look appreciatively at him as he strode towards her.

'How did you get down here?'

The peremptory demand was curt and to the point.

'I called a cab.'

He was frowning.

'You could have asked me to drive you.'

She gave him a bitterly angry look and started to turn away from him without responding.

Immediately he placed a restraining hand on her arm.

'I said—'

'I heard what you said.' Carly stopped him. 'And for your information I would have walked here—barefoot, if necessary—rather than ask you for help.'

A cautionary inner voice tried to remind her that she had decided to behave towards him with cool professionalism.

'The wounded pride effect won't cut any ice with me, Carly,' he told her. 'I see you've managed to acquire a change of clothes,' he added dryly.

No way was she going to tell him that the cost of the taxi plus these clothes had taken all but a few of her small store of euros, and that without the money she had got from pawning her watch right now she would have had less than the cost of a cup of coffee and a sandwich in her bag. She pulled away from him instead.

A small commotion on the yacht's walkway had her turning round to watch Mariella D'Argent, flanked by sundry members of her personal staff, walking towards them.

The ex-model looked stunning. She was wearing close-fitting Capri pants low on the hips to reveal an enviably taut flat stomach and hipbones. A contrasting halter-necked top skimmed the perfect, if somewhat suspiciously unmoving shape of her breasts, which were obviously bare beneath it. A large straw hat and a pair of huge dark sunglasses shielded her face from the sunlight, and on her feet she was wearing a pair of impossibly flimsy high-heeled sandals.

She ignored Carly, smiling warmly at Ricardo instead and exclaiming excitedly, 'Ricardo, darling—how wonderful. I didn't know you were in St Tropez. You must join us tonight. We're having a small party to launch the new yacht.'

Carly watched as Ricardo smiled his acceptance without saying that he had already intended to be present.

'And you must come to the dinner we're having first—just a select few of us.'

Behind Mariella's back Sarah caught Carly's eye and pulled a face.

'What are you doing now?' Mariella was asking. 'We're all on our way to Nikki Beach. Why don't you come with us?'

'I don't think so, Mariella,' Carly heard Ricardo reply firmly. 'I'm afraid I've outgrown the appeal of paying a hugely inflated sum of money to buy a bottle of champagne to spray all over some so-called model's equally hugely inflated chest.'

Mariella gave a small trill of laughter—which was quite an impressive feat, since not a single muscle in her face moved as she did so, Carly reflected, then pulled herself up mentally for being a bitch.

'That won't please her,' Sarah muttered to Carly as she came to stand next to her. 'And she's already in a strop because *Hello!* magazine has pulled out of giving the party a double-page spread. It's doing one on some film star's new nursery instead. Who's the hunk, by the way?' she whispered, looking at Ricardo.

'A potential new client,' Carly answered her. 'He wants to see the way we work.'

'Mmm, well, he's certainly brightened Mariella's day for her. What's the betting she's already planning how to lure him down to her stateroom and which Agent Provocateur underwear she's going to be wearing when she does?'

'I don't think she'll have to try very hard,' Carly answered lightly. 'They seem very much two of a kind.'

So why was she suffering such a wrenching pain at the thought of them together?

It was physical frustration, that was all, she reassured herself as she continued to ignore Ricardo, keeping her back turned towards him. Because after the pang of longing that had come through her when she had seen him striding towards her she didn't trust herself to be able to look directly at him.

From the table where he was sitting at a café opposite the harbour, Ricardo had an uninterrupted view of the D'Argents' yacht and the activity around it being orchestrated by Carly.

It was true that last night he had been too enraged and frustrated to think analytically about the way she was likely to react to his denunciation of her, and it was also true that, had he done so, it certainly wouldn't have occurred to him that she would retreat behind a screen of icy politeness and professionalism. On the one hand meticulously making sure that he was provided with ample opportunity to witness every aspect of the preparations for the upcoming event and ask whatever questions he wished, and yet on the other managing to convey to him very clearly that she loathed and resented every second she had to spend in his company.

As a portrayal of an affronted woman whose morals were beyond reproach it was very impressive, he admitted. Unfortunately for her, though, he knew she was no such thing. So she was wasting her time.

It was irritating that Prêt a Party's financial year-end meant that the only figures available for his inspection were virtually a year out of date. He had given instructions that he wanted more up to date financial information, but that, of course, would take time as it would have to be acquired discreetly. He certainly did not want anyone else alerted to the fact that he was considering it as an acquisition.

He picked up the local newspaper a previous occupant of the table had left and opened it. Italian was his first language, but he was fluent in several others, including French. He was idly flicking through the pages when a sentimentally captioned photograph on one of them caught his eye. Frowning, he studied it in disbelief.

An 'angel of mercy', the paper fancifully described a young woman holding out sandwiches to a group of beggar children. The photo accompanied a piece on the best ways to help street children, and the woman was quite definitely Carly, even if she had been photographed with her back to the camera. He also recognised the airport location, and the suitcase on the ground behind her—although not the outstretched male hand that was just in the shot, grasping it.

He closed the paper, his mouth grim.

Okay, so maybe—just maybe—her suitcase had genuinely been stolen. As for her act of charity... He hadn't missed the way she had reached out to the smallest and weakest of the children, making sure that he received his fair share of the food she was handing out. As a boy he had had first-hand experience of what it was like to have to beg for food.

A large limousine drew up in front of Carly and several people got out and started to walk towards her. One of them she recognised as the current 'in' classical violinist who had been hired to play as the guests came on board.

Immediately she went to greet him and introduce herself to him and his entourage. The violinist, unlike the catering staff and the florist, had been invited to mingle with the guests later in the evening, and had been given a room in a St Tropez luxurious boutique hotel, paid for by the D'Argents.

Naturally he wanted to know where he would be playing, and dutifully Carly set about answering his manager's questions.

Inside she was still feeling sick with shock and misery over Ricardo's accusations, but she was here to do a job, not indulge her own feelings. And besides, she had a long history of having to hide what she was feeling and the pain and humiliation others had inflicted on her.

Her adoptive parents might turn to her for financial assistance, but it had been their own daughter to whom they had given their love, not Carly.

Ricardo got up and came towards Carly.

'I'm going back to the villa shortly. Presumably you

will wish to go back yourself at some stage, in order to get ready for this evening. Should you want a lift—'

'I don't,' Carly told him curtly, without looking up from checking one of the invoices in front of her.

'Cut out the hard-done-by act, Carly,' Ricardo snapped, equally curtly. 'I'm not taken in by it.'

'I don't wish to discuss it.'

'You thought you'd fooled me and you don't like the fact that I caught you out.'

'No. What I don't like is the fact that I was stupid enough to think there was anything remotely desirable about you.'

'But you did desire me, didn't you?'

'You must excuse me, Mr Salvatore. I've got work to do.'

She didn't turn to watch him as he walked away from her, but nevertheless she knew immediately when he had gone.

'How's it going?'

Carly gave Sarah, the PA, a slightly harassed smile.

'Okay! So far there's only been one major fall-out between the chefs.'

Sarah laughed. 'You're lucky,' she announced, 'You can add a zero to that so far as the D'Argent's are concerned. Not that *they* fall out so much as *she* falls out with *him*! Did you manage to find something to wear for later?'

Carly shook her head. 'I haven't had time,' she told her truthfully.

'Would these be any use, then?' Sarah asked her, pointing to the overstuffed bin liner she had just put down.

'It's some stuff Mariella told me to get rid of ages

ago. Look at this—it would be perfect for you for to-night,' she announced, whipping a mass of silk black fabric out of the top of the bin liner. 'It's a sort of top and palazzo pants thing, all in one.'

The fine silk floated mouthwateringly through Carly's fingers. 'Are you sure that Mariella won't mind?' she asked Sarah worriedly.

'I doubt she'll even notice. Not once she hits the champagne and cocaine,' Sarah answered bluntly.

'It's very sheer...' Carly hesitated.

'You can wear a body underneath it—although Mariella didn't. Oh, and you'll need a pair of high heels—you should be able to pick something up at the market whilst they're having dinner. And if you can't get away you can use my cabin to shower and get changed in.'

Carly gave her a grateful look of relief. 'I was won-dering how one earth I was going to manage to make time for that,' she admitted. 'I daren't leave the chefs alone together for too long, and I've promised Jeff I'll make sure no one touches his box trees!'

Sarah laughed and shook her head. 'When is my prince going to come and take me away from all this?' She sighed.

CHAPTER SIX

'HERE they come...'

Carly gave Sarah a slightly distracted smile as they both watched the long line of limousines queuing up to disgorge the D'Argents' guests.

Carly had changed into the black outfit Sarah had given her, and was self-consciously aware of how very suggestively revealing it was. Not even the flesh-coloured body she was wearing beneath it could totally offset the effect of the layers of sheer black fabric floating around her body, revealing with every movement the sensual gleam of her skin beneath the silk.

If she had had something else to wear she would have done so. Sarah had intended to be kind, Carly knew, but no way was this outfit, with its tight-fitting top and hip-hugging palazzo pants bottom, suitable as discreet 'work wear'. But the other outfits had been just as bad.

Already as people approached the gangway they were looking at her—especially the men, some of whom were giving her openly lascivious glances.

Two over-chunky and businesslike dinner-suited bouncer types were checking the invitations before allowing guests to step forward into the open-fronted enclosure, where uniformed staff were waiting to offer welcome glasses of champagne cocktail. The glasses were arranged on white trays, whilst the cocktails were a steel-grey colour.

'What on earth is in them?' Carly had whispered to their own *maître d'*.

'Champagne, liqueur and colouring,' he had told her dryly. 'Mariella D'Argent was insistent that they had to be grey!'

Prior to the D'Argents' return Carly had made a swift inspection of the yacht's receptions areas, to check that everything was as it should be. Privately she felt that the glass floor over thousands of small white lights was a bit OTT, but she had been assured that it was nothing compared with what some people asked for.

The violinist had begun to play, the dinner guests had returned, and Mariella had gone to her suite to get changed into her specially commissioned outfit.

A posse of older men and their too-young arm candy were arriving, the girls all wearing similar teeny-weenie, heavily embroidered clinging dresses and tottering on too-high heels. They were all obviously bleached blondes. Carly suppressed a small sigh.

More guests were arriving, and Carly recognised amongst them some very A-list celebrities—a famous actress, the daughter of a pop icon, a couple of ex-models—all of them accompanied by good-looking men.

But Ricardo hadn't arrived as yet. Not that she was looking for him!

'I'd better go in and be on hand, just in case Mariella wants me for anything,' Sarah whispered to her.

Nodding her head, Carly continued to keep a discreet watch on the arrivals.

'We're going to run short of cocktails any minute,' the *maître d'* muttered warningly.

It took over an hour for all the guests to arrive, by which time Carly was downstairs in the main salon, keeping an eye on the proceedings there and trying to avoid getting too close to Mariella—just in case she should object to Carly wearing her discarded outfit!

Drugs were being passed round openly, and the sound of laughter was growing louder as they began to take effect.

Already some of the guests had started to behave recklessly. A well-known media mogul had grabbed a girl almost in front of Carly and now proceeded to caress her intimately whilst the girl herself encouraged him.

This was just not a lifestyle with which she felt comfortable, Carly reflected with revulsion. She couldn't understand how anyone could find any pleasure in something that ultimately was so very destructive. Drugs were anathema to her. Her eyes shadowed as she remembered how she had seen the misery that they could cause.

She felt a tug on her arm and turned to see one of the older men leering at her. She'd realised from overhearing them talking earlier that they were Russian.

'You come with me,' he demanded drunkenly.

'I'm sorry, I'm not a guest. I'm working,' Carly told him politely, trying to disengage herself.

'Good, then you work for me...in bed,' he responded coarsely. 'I pay you good, eh?'

Carly felt nauseated. Was that how all men saw women—as someone, *something* they could buy? A commodity they could use? Or did she attract that type because somehow instinctively they could sense what she had come from?

Trash! She winced as though she had been knifed, hearing again the contemptuous word that had been thrown at her so often during her childhood.

'You are trash, do you know that? Garbage. In fact,

that's where they found you—lying in the rubbish, unwanted—and that's where you should have stayed.'

Abruptly she realised that she could feel the man's
hot breath on her bare skin.

She turned to demand that he release her, and then
tensed. Ricardo was standing on the other side of the
salon, watching her.

He knew what she was, Ricardo reminded himself
savagely, so why did the sight of Carly allowing another
man to hold her arm so intimately fill him with jealousy
instead of contempt? And why the hell was he now
pushing his way through the crowd milling through the
salon, in the wake of the D'Argents, in order to get to
her? After all, he had already seen the proprietorial way
her male companion had reached for her. And what was
driving him through the crowd certainly wasn't rooted
in some kind of male solidarity, or an altruistic desire
to warn her latest victim of just what she was, was it?
He derided himself cynically. The truth was, he preferred not to analyse just what the sight of another man
holding on to her was doing to him—or why.

Instead he channelled his anger into deciding that her
escort's taste in clothes—for obviously he must have
bought her the abomination she was wearing—was
about as good as Carly's was in men. The pair of them
deserved one another, and Carly deserved everything
she would get from selling herself to a man who might
just as well have had what he was tattooed across his
forehead.

But Carly wasn't here to have a relationship with
another man, and he intended to remind her in no uncertain terms that *he* was supposed to be her prime concern. How dared she reject him and then let that over-
weight, sweaty nobody put his greasy hands all over

her? Where was her pride? Her self-respect? Didn't it ever occur to her that she was intelligent enough to earn her own living and support herself, instead of debasing herself by offering herself to any man who would give her the price of a few designer rags?

'You! Here!'

Carly stared at the man who had spoken to her so arrogantly as he approached, and then realised that he was with the man who was holding her.

'How much do you want?'

He was already opening his wallet and starting to remove money from it.

Another man had joined the other two, taller and leaner, and with an unmistakable air of authority about him. He spoke sharply to them, and to Carly's relief she was immediately released.

'I apologise for my countrymen—I hope you will not condemn all Russian men as unmannerly oafs because of them?'

He was charming, and very good-looking, Carly acknowledged.

'Of course not,' she assured him.

'You are here alone?'

Someone pushed past and he reached out a protective arm to shield her. Unexpectedly Carly suddenly felt very femininely weak and vulnerable. She wasn't used to men behaving protectively towards her.

'I'm with the event planning organisation,' she explained.

'Ah, so you are responsible for this magnificent party we are enjoying?'

He was flattering as well as charming, Carly recognised.

'In part,' she agreed.

'And you are staying here, on board the yacht?'

'No, I'm—' Carly broke off as she saw both Sarah and the *maître d'* edging towards her. 'Please excuse me,' she apologised to him. 'But I must get back to work.'

'Mmm, I see Igor was chatting you up. Mariella won't like that,' Sarah warned Carly, when she joined her, having dealt with the *maître d'*. 'She's already got him marked down as husband number four. Mind you, she'll have her work cut out, because she certainly isn't the only woman who's hoping for a legal right to his billions. God, I hate these dos,' Sarah complained. 'Sometimes I wonder why the hell I don't just give in my notice and go home.'

'Why don't you?' Carly asked her

'Let's just say there's a man there who I can't have,' Sarah told her bleakly. 'I need another drink. I'll be back in a minute…'

Carly was standing with her back to him, watching Sarah hurry away from her, when Ricardo finally managed to reach her.

'Lost your new admirer?'

Carly stiffened, and then turned round reluctantly to face him.

Before she could defend herself, he continued savagely, 'What the hell possessed you to let him buy you that? You look like a tart,' he told her mercilessly. 'Or was that the idea? It certainly looked as though he was doing a brisk business in selling you on to his friends.'

Carly's face burned. 'You are despicable,' she told him. 'And for your information—'

'Ricardo, darling—there you are!'

Although she was delighted to have Ricardo's attention removed from her, Carly couldn't help wishing that the woman claiming it was not Mariella—especially when she saw the way Mariella was staring at her outfit.

Fortunately, though, before she could say anything Sarah returned. Equally fortunately, she immediately realised what was happening and adroitly came to Carly's rescue, exclaiming, 'Mariella! Carly hasn't been able to stop singing your praises for being so kind to her and saving her so much embarrassment. I told her that it is typical of you to be so generous, and that you'd understand immediately how she felt about having her suitcase stolen. I knew you wouldn't mind if I let her borrow those old things you told me to put to one side for the charity shop. Remember? You said they were too big for you...'

Was it the weight of false sentiment and sugar in Sarah's paean of praise that miraculously squashed the hostility in Mariella's gaze? Carly wondered cynically. Suddenly she became all gracious smiles.

'Of course. I love helping other people—everyone knows that. Although I must say you are rather too big to fit into my things, my dear. Of course I am very slim,' she added smugly, before ignoring Carly to turn to Ricardo and say prettily, 'Ricardo, why don't I introduce you to a few more people...?'

As Mariella drew Ricardo away Sarah exhaled and apologised to Carly.

'I hope you didn't mind me saying that—only she looked as though she was about to create a bit of a scene...'

'No, I didn't mind at all,' Carly assured her truthfully. But she would have loved to see Ricardo's face if Mariella had claimed ownership of her outfit when he had been in the middle of insulting it. Although he hadn't merely insulted the outfit, had he? He'd insulted her as well.

She didn't care what he thought about her, Carly assured herself. After all, she knew the truth and she knew that he was wrong. At least this way, even if she couldn't deny or ignore the physical, sexual effect he had on her, she knew she would be safe from any risk of becoming emotionally attracted to him.

Not, of course, that she *had* been in any danger of that.

It seemed as if the evening was never going to end, Carly thought wearily. The last of the guests had finally gone, but she and the others were still cleaning up.

'Look, why don't you go? There's nothing more for you to do here,' Jeff the florist said in a kind voice.

'It's my responsibility to stay until everything is packed up,' Carly told him.

'You don't think that anyone else would stay around this long, do you?' He grinned at her and shook his head. 'We're perfectly capable of sorting what's left, and besides…' He was looking past her and she turned her head to see what he was looking at.

Her heart gave a sudden heavy thud as the door of the car which had drawn up a few yards away opened and Ricardo got out.

The last time she'd seen him he had been deep in conversation with a stunning redhead whom she was sure she had heard murmuring something about going back to her hotel suite with her. So what was he doing back here now?

Why should the fact that he was striding so purposefully towards her make her legs and her will-power quiver with weakness? He had insulted her in the most offensive way possible, and yet here she was letting his sexuality and, even worse, her own reaction to it, get to her.

Maybe she should adopt a different and more modern attitude. After all, she had heard plenty of women say openly and unashamedly that they were up for having sex with a man without wanting or needing any kind of emotional connection with him. Surely that kind of relationship was exactly what would suit her best?

'It's gone three a.m. and we leave for New York in the morning,' he told her curtly.

'You go, Carly,' Jeff repeated. 'We can easily finish up here now.'

It seemed that she didn't have any choice. Turning aside, Carly went to retrieve the canvas hold-all she had bought earlier to hold her modest new purchases.

She watched with a certain sense of grim satisfaction as Ricardo frowned and took it from her.

'Before you say anything,' she warned him coolly, when they were out of Jeff's hearing, 'I didn't have to sell my body to buy either the bag or its contents. What happened to the redhead, by the way?' she asked unkindly as they walked back to the car. The fact that Ricardo was a potential client had been overwhelmed by her still smarting pride. 'Didn't she come up to your expectations—or was it you who didn't come up to hers?'

'Neither. She left with the man with whom she arrived—and even if she hadn't *I* don't take those kinds of risks with my health,' Ricardo answered pointedly.

He was opening the car door for her, but Carly paused to turn round and demand angrily, 'Meaning what? That I do? Isn't the discovery that you've already made one offensive and insulting error of judgement about me enough?'

Without waiting for his response she got into the car, ignoring him as she reached for the seatbelt, and continuing to ignore him when he walked round the car, climbed into the driver's seat and started the car engine.

They reached the villa. Carly opened the car door and got out without waiting for Ricardo to help her.

The pink-washed building was bathed in a soft rose glow from the artfully placed nightscape lighting, which illuminated both the villa and its gardens. Rose-pink—the colour of romance. A small, painful smile twisted her lips.

'Carly.'

She stopped walking and turned to look as Ricardo caught up with her.

'Why didn't you tell me that the outfit you were wearing belonged to Mariella?'

'Perhaps I didn't want to spoil your fun. You were obviously enjoying thinking the worst of me,' she answered sharply.

'You can't blame me for making entirely logical assumptions. You're a woman in her twenties with a career, therefore logically you must have a bank account. Having a bank account means that you have access to credit cards, bank loans, a wide variety of different ways of borrowing money in an emergency—as this—' he indicated the bag he was now carrying '—proves. And yet you chose to ask me for a loan.'

'Logical assumptions? You've already as good as admitted that the assumptions you've made about me, far from being logical, are based entirely on your own preconceived ideas and personal hang-ups. The truth is that you know nothing whatsoever about my life or my circumstances. If the women you mix with are the type who are happy to exchange sex for a few gaudy trinkets and a wardrobe of designer clothes, then I'm afraid that so far as I'm concerned it says just as much about your judgement and morals as it does about theirs.'

'Really? Well, *my* judgement told me that you were more than ready to have sex with me until you found out that sex was all you would be getting. Miraculously, now that you know that, suddenly you have all the money you need to replace your stolen clothes. Oh, and a word of warning. That gang are notorious for wanting value for their money. They'll pass you round from hand to hand and have all they want of you. You may not find it worth the pay.'

No one had ever made her feel so furiously angry. She was so angry, in fact, that for once she forgot her normal caution and instead burst out, 'You are so wrong. The only reason I was ready to have sex with you was because I wanted you—but, luckily for me, I wanted to retain my self-respect more. And as for my bank account and my new clothes—I asked you for a loan because I have had to empty my bank account to…to make my parents a…a loan. I do not own a credit card, since I disapprove of their punitively high rates of interest, and there wasn't time for me to realise any of my assets.'

Ricardo frowned. Surely no one could manufacture the level of fury Carly was showing? But he wasn't simply going to give in.

'But obviously somehow you managed to find some money?'

'Yes, but not by selling my body, as you so obviously would like to think.'

'No? How, then?' The cynical disbelief in his voice infuriated her.

'If you must know—not that it is any of your business—I pawned my watch,' she told him flatly.

Ricardo discovered that a sensation akin to the slow, measured drip of ice being fed straight into his bloodstream was creeping up over him—a mental awareness that somehow he had got something very important spectacularly wrong.

He couldn't remember the last time anyone had wrongfooted him, and the knowledge that it should be Carly who had done so sparked off inside him a very dangerous cocktail of emotions. He looked down at her bare wrist and then back at her face.

'You said your parents needed a loan? Surely you could—'

'I don't want to talk about it.' Carly cut him off quickly.

Ricardo frowned. Surely the kind of woman he had assumed her to be would have been only too eager to make much of the glow of virtue accruing to her from such selflessness. But Carly was turning away from him, quite plainly agitated and anxious to change the subject.

Why? Ricardo wondered. What on earth could there be about something as generous as lending money to one's parents to spark off the hostility and fear he could see so plainly in her eyes?

She was starting to walk away from him. He looked down at her wrist again, and then back at her face.

He had always trusted his instincts, and right now those instincts were insisting that Carly had been telling him the truth. Therefore he was guilty of seriously misjudging her. And his body was telling him that, no matter what she was or what she had done or not done, he wanted her.

He strode towards her, catching hold of her arm.

Immediately her whole body tensed, and she demanded fiercely, 'Let go of me.'

'Not yet. You aren't the only one who takes their moral responsibilities seriously. I obviously owe you an apology.'

Ricardo was actually apologising to her? He certainly needed to, she reminded herself angrily. And she needed to apologise to herself, for being so stupid as to actually still want him.

'Yes, you do,' she agreed coolly. 'But I don't want it.'

She watched his stunned disbelief give way to male anger.

'No? But you do want me, don't you?' he taunted softly.

'No,' she began, but it was already too late. He pulled her hard against him and bent his head to take her mouth in a savagely intimate kiss before she could object. And, of course, the moment his mouth touched hers, her own helpless response betrayed her. She tried to pull away but he held on to her, and her eyes widened as she saw in his eyes the same hunger she knew was in her own.

She made a small helpless sound of denial and need, and then she gave in. His mouth moved urgently on hers and her lips parted eagerly, greedily for its possession, her nails digging into the hard muscles of his arms as her need roared through her.

It was last night all over again—only this time they were impeded by two sets of clothes. She had changed back into her own things before supervising the clearing up after the party. Now she was being driven wild by her longing to be as naked and open to him now as she had been the previous evening.

Her fingers clenched spasmodically on his arm, her body gripped by savage shudders of dark pleasure.

She wanted his hands on her breasts, on *all* of her—his fingers finding her, touching her as they had done last night. Just wanting him to touch her in that way made her go hot and limp with the desire she could feel pulsing inside her. She wanted him there…there—deep, deep inside her, thrusting hard and fast against the possessive hold of her muscles, taking her, satisfying her quickly and mercilessly.

She could feel the open heat of his mouth against her throat as he tipped her back over his arm, moonlight gleaming whitely on her skin as he tugged off her top to reveal her breast, darkly crowned in the night light.

His thumb-tip rubbed against the deep dark pink of her nipple and she cried out—a sharp, agonised sound of primitive female mating hunger.

She wanted him to take her now, here. As quickly and completely, as fiercely and thoroughly as a panting she-creature on heat. She wanted him to fill her, flood her with his own release, and to go on doing so until she was sated and complete.

She reached for the hardness she knew was waiting for her, running her fingers over and over the jutting ridge of his erection, quivering with anticipation. The head would be swollen and hot, the body thick and darkly veined, the flesh tightly drawn over the hard muscle, but still fluid and slick when she touched it.

In her imagination she could already feel the first rub of that engorged head between the lips of her sex, and then against the sensitive pleasure-pulse of her clitoris over and over again, faster and faster, until she was wet and hot with her pleasure. Until she could endure no more and Ricardo finally plunged deep inside her.

As though she had cried her desire out loud to him, she felt Ricardo tugging at her clothes, his hands hard and firm against her naked skin. His mouth found her nipple and drew fiercely on it. She cried out again in a mewling sound of intense arousal.

His mouth returned to hers. She felt as though she had been starving for it, for him, as though she had been waiting all their life to be with him. She felt...

Immediately she tensed, pushing him away, her voice tight with rejection and self-loathing as she told him fiercely, 'I don't want this.'

'Yes, you do. You want this and you want me, and you can't deny it!' Ricardo challenged her whilst he fought to control his breathing. And to rationalise what had happened—if he could rationalise it. It was something he had had no intention of allowing to happen at all. But from the moment he had touched her he had been out of control, unable to stop what was happening to him.

Carly drew in a deep, shaky breath.

'We mustn't.'

'We must not what?' Ricardo demanded. 'We must not want one another?'

Carly turned her head away from him and shook it in bewilderment. 'This can't happen again,' she told him quickly.

Baffled and frustrated, Ricardo reluctantly let her go. She wanted him, and he certainly damned well wanted her, so why was she behaving like this? One thing he did know was that he was determined that he would have her, sooner or later—and he would prefer it to be sooner.

Thank heavens Ricardo hadn't followed her to her room. Because if he had she knew that she would not have been able to resist him. And she had to resist him, because she wanted him far more than it was safe for her to do.

Why, though, did she feel like this about him? Why did she want him when she had never wanted any of the other men she had met?

Was it because subconsciously she knew he was different from them? Because the most intimate part of her recognised that, at some primal level, she felt a deep-rooted kinship with him?

Because, like him, she too had known and suffered childhood poverty and the withdrawal, the denial of the love and nurturing, the protection every child should be given as of right?

The wretched squalor and unhappiness of her own early childhood had marked her for ever, as she knew his must have marked him.

Not even Julia and Lucy, who thought they knew everything about her, knew the full truth of the beginning of her life—how she had been found dressed in rags, abandoned in the street beside some rubbish, her pitiful cries alerting a loitering tramp to her existence.

She had been a piece of unwanted humanity, left there to die. Unwanted and unloved, even by her own birth mother. No wonder, then, that her adopted mother had never been able to love her either.

CHAPTER SEVEN

'YOU mentioned last night that you didn't have any money in your bank account because you'd had to help your parents?'

Carly almost dropped the glass of water she had been drinking. A little unsteadily, she put it down. They had boarded Ricardo's jet several hours later than Ricardo had originally planned, although he had not give her any reason for the delay, and would soon be landing at JFK airport for their onward journey to the Hamptons.

She looked out of the window, telling herself that it was pointless now to berate herself for letting anger lead her into admitting that she had needed to help them.

'I…I shouldn't have said that,' she admitted uncomfortably. 'And I wouldn't have done if you hadn't made me so angry.'

'I misjudged you, and I've apologised for that. A man in my position becomes very cynical about other people's motives. Why did you have to give your parents money? Are you an only child?'

'I…I had a sister…'

Her mouth had gone dry, and she wanted desperately to bring their conversation to an end.

'Had?' Ricardo questioned, as she had known he would.

'Yes. She… Fenella died a…a few months ago,' she told him reluctantly.

Ricardo could almost feel her resistance to his questions as he registered her words and felt the shock of them, plus his own shock that she should be so composed.

'I'm sorry. That must have been dreadful for you.'

Carly looked at him.

'Fenella and I weren't really related. I…her parents adopted me when I was very young. They adored her, and they were naturally devastated by her death,' she told him in a guarded voice.

'But you weren't?' Ricardo guessed.

'We were very different. Fenella naturally was always the favoured child. Adoption doesn't always work out the way people hope it will.'

Carly looked away from him. It was obvious that she was withholding something from him, *withdrawing* herself from him, in fact—as though she didn't want to let him into the personal side of her life. To his own astonishment he discovered that he didn't like the fact that she was reluctant to talk openly about herself to him. What was it about her that caused him to have this compulsion to learn more? And was it more, or was it *everything* there was to learn?

His curiosity was merely that of a potential employer, he assured himself.

'What do you mean, adoption doesn't always work? Didn't it work for you? Weren't you happy with your adoptive parents?'

'Why are you asking me so many questions?'

Ricardo could almost feel her anxiety and panic.

'Perhaps because I want to know more about you.'

On the face of it he already knew all he needed to know. But it was what was beneath the surface that was arousing his curiosity. She was concealing something from him, something that changed her from a self-confident woman into someone who was far more vulnerable—and also very determined to deny that vulnerability. He had a fiercely honed instinct about such things, and he knew he wasn't wrong. So what was it? He intended to find out. But what would it take to break down her barriers?

He looked at her and watched in satisfaction as, under his deliberate scrutiny, the colour seeped up under her skin.

'You haven't answered my question,' he reminded her.

'No, I wasn't happy.' The terseness in her voice warned him that she didn't like his probing.

'What about your natural parents?'

Ricardo could see immediately that his question had had a very dramatic effect on her. Her face lost its colour and he could hear her audibly indrawn breath. He expected her to refuse to answer, but instead she spoke fiercely.

'My mother was probably a drug addict, who died in a house fire along with two other young women. No one knew who my father might have been. I was left to die amongst the rubbish outside a hospital. A tramp found me. I was only a few weeks old. I was ten years old and in foster care when Fenella's parents decided they wanted to adopt a sister for her, because they were concerned that she might be lonely.'

Ricardo was frowning.

'They adopted you for their daughter?'

'Yes. I imagine they felt I'd be easier to house-train than a puppy and less expensive to keep than a pony,' Carly told him lightly. 'Unfortunately, though, it didn't work out. Fenella, quite naturally, hated having to share her parents and her toys with an unwanted sibling, and demanded that her parents send me back. I think they wanted to, but of course it was too late. I wasn't allowed to touch anything of Fenella's, or even to eat in the same room with her at first. But then we were both sent to boarding school. That's when I met Jules and Lucy. Somehow or other my...my history, and the fact that I wasn't really Fenella's sister, became public knowledge.'

'You mean she told everyone?' Ricardo asked bluntly.

'She was a year older than me, so she'd already made her own circle of friends at the school before I went there. She was a very popular girl—she could be charming when she wanted to be—and I very quickly became ostracised.'

'You were bullied, you mean?'

'I was different and I didn't fit in,' Carly continued without answering him. 'But luckily for me, Jules and Lucy came to my rescue and gave me their friendship. Without that and them...' The shadows in her eyes caused Ricardo to experience a sudden fierce surge of protectiveness towards her, and anger towards those who had so obviously tormented her.

'What happened to Fenella?'

Carly shook her head. It disturbed her to realise how much she had told him about herself.

She wasn't going to tell him any more, Ricardo recognised, as he watched her turn away from him to focus on her laptop.

Carly frowned as she tried to study the figures on the company's bank statements on her screen. Answering Ricardo's questions had brought back so many painful memories.

She had truly believed when she had been adopted that she was going to be loved by her new parents and

sister, and she had given them her own love unstint-
ingly. It had confused her at first when she had been
rebuffed, but then she had seen her adoptive mother
hugging Fenella, fussing over her, and she had begun
to realise that there was a huge difference between the
way Fenella was given her parents' love and approval,
and the way she was refused it.

She had tried to make herself as like Fenella as possible, mirroring the other girl's behaviour as closely as
she could, assuming that this would gain her adoptive
parents' approval. Instead it had simply made Fenella
hate her even more. Now, as an adult, she could not
entirely blame them. Fenella had been their child, after
all. But her experience with her adoptive parents had
taught her the danger of giving her love to anyone.

The figures in front of her blurred, and she had to
blink fiercely in order to be able to concentrate on them.

Suddenly, when she saw them properly, she frowned,
firmly putting her own problems to one side as she
stared in shocked anxiety at the unfamiliarly large
cheques that had gone through the account, almost completely emptying it of cash.

It was unthinkable that this should have happened.
She prided herself on keeping a mental running total of
what was going in and out of the account, and according
to her own mental reckoning they should have been
several hundred thousand pounds in credit. In fact, they
needed to be several hundred thousand pounds in credit
to meet the bills their suppliers would be presenting at
the end of the month, and to leave sufficient working
capital to carry them until they received payment from
other clients.

So what were these cheques for? She couldn't remember signing them. A cold trickle of anxiety mixed

with instinct iced down her spine. Her heart started to beat uncomfortably heavily. She needed to see those cheques.

Carly had quickly become totally engrossed in her work. Too quickly, Ricardo thought. Did she use it to block out emotional issues she found it difficult to handle? She had not said so, but he imagined that she must have suffered severe emotional trauma during her childhood.

That he should even have such a concern, never mind actively feel protective of her because of it, was such alien emotional territory to him that it took several seconds to recognise his own danger. Once he had done so he reminded himself firmly that that had been then and this was now, and now he wanted her in his bed.

Carly ordered photocopies of the cheques. Until they came she wouldn't be able to do anything else.

'Carly!'

She acknowledged Ricardo with a wary look.

'I hope you ached as much for me last night as I did for you.'

She could feel her face starting to burn.

'I'd really rather not talk about it. I've already said that I don't want to…to go there.'

Her voice was calm, but he could see that her hand was trembling.

He gave a small shrug.

'Why not? Why should we deny ourselves something it's obvious we both want? Sexually there's a chemistry between us that maybe neither of us would have wanted, given free choice, but I don't see any point in trying to pretend that it doesn't exist. And, given that it does exist, perhaps it would be better for both of us if we enjoyed it instead of trying to ignore or reject it.

That way at least we could get our sexual hunger for one another out of our systems.'

Our sexual hunger. Three simple words. But they had the power to change her life for ever. Had Adam felt what she was feeling now when Eve had handed him the apple and announced, 'Here, take a bite?' Had he thought then, just as she was thinking now, of all that he would be denying himself if he refused? If she had sex with Ricardo it wouldn't change the world, but it would change her. Was she brave enough to accept that? Or would she rather spend the rest of her life wishing and wondering?

'I don't want to have an affair with you,' she answered him. An affair would involve falling in love, putting herself in a situation where ultimately she would be rejected in favour of someone else. Every emotional experience she'd ever had had taught her that. In her foster homes, with her adoptive parents, and then at school. Even with her closest friends, Lucy and Jules, she was aware that they shared an extra special bond of birth and upbringing which excluded her.

'But you do want to have sex with me,' Ricardo guessed.

Her face was burning, but she managed to hold his gaze.

'I...I think so.'

The look he gave her was pure male power.

'Are you asking me to make the decision for you?'

'What would be the point? I'm sure a man with your experience could find someone else who wouldn't need to have a decision made for them.'

'I'm sure I could,' Ricardo agreed dryly. 'However, they would not be you, and it is you I want. But, since

we're on the subject of relationships, how many relationships *have* there been for you?'

He had caught her unprepared, slipping the question
under her guard.

'Er… I don't… I can't really remember,' she told
him untruthfully. 'And besides, it isn't really any of
your business, is it?'

'It would be if we slept together,' Ricardo told her.

How could she tell him the truth?

How could she say that he was different—special—
that she had never felt the way she did about him with
anyone else, and that that alone was enough to make
her feel threatened and afraid? And if she couldn't tell
him that, then how could she tell him that she had never
done with anyone else what she so much wanted to do
with him?

'What time do you think we will arrive at the
Hamptons?' she asked instead.

The look he gave her made her feel as though he had
set a match to her will-power and it was curling up into
nothing inside her.

'We'll be there in plenty of time. We'll stay over in
my New York apartment tonight and fly out tomorrow.'

'Wouldn't it make more sense to go straight there?'

'Not really. You're looking and sounding very agitated, Carly. Why?'

'No reason. I mean, I'm not. Why should I be?'

'Perhaps you don't feel you can trust yourself to be
alone with me?' Ricardo suggested softly.

Carly had had enough.

'It isn't a matter of that! I just don't think we should
put ourselves in a position where—'

'Where what? Where you might be tempted to offer

yourself to me and I might accept? Is that what you mean?'

'No! At least...' That was exactly what she had meant, she admitted to herself. Only in her mental scenario it had been Ricardo offering himself to her, not the other way around.

Something about the way he had phrased his statement touched a raw nerve. 'I don't like what you're implying,' she told him frankly. 'I appreciate that lots of women probably come on to you because...'

'Because I'm very rich?' he suggested smoothly, picking up her dropped sentence.

His voice might sound smooth, but beneath it he was angry, Carly recognised. He might not feel concerned about her sensitivities, but he obviously did not like her treading on his own!

'I wasn't going to say that.'

'Liar!' Ricardo told her, adding coolly,

'Besides, there are always several components to sexual desire, surely? For instance there are those which relate to our senses—sight, scent, taste...touch...'

Carly could feel herself beginning to respond to each word that rolled off his tongue.

Yes, the sight of him aroused her, and his scent certainly did, and as for his taste... She pulled in her stomach muscles to try and control the ache spreading through her. And touch... She pulled them in tighter, but it was already too late to halt what she was feeling. And, yes, the sound of his voice as well...

'And then there are those that relate to personality, status...lifestyle. For instance—' He broke off as the steward emerged from the crew's quarters and came towards them.

Carly could feel herself shaking slightly inside—the sensual effect on her body from just listening to him.

'We'll be landing in half an hour. Would you like another drink before we do? Or something to eat?'

Carly shook her head, unable to trust herself to speak. Ricardo had dragged from her confidences and admissions she would normally never have made to anyone, and right now emotional reaction was beginning to set in—much the same way as physical reaction would have set in if she had just had a tooth pulled without anaesthetic. She felt slightly sick, more than slightly shaky, and very much in shock.

Perhaps Ricardo was right, and the only way to overcome her physical ache for him was to satisfy it instead of trying to avoid it.

Ricardo watched her, shielding his scrutiny with a pretended concentration on his own papers. Over and over again she broke out of the stereotyped image he wanted to impose on her. No other woman had shown him—given him—*shared* with him—such an intensity of sexual desire. And no other woman had ever aroused him to such a point of compelling compulsive hunger either.

They were coming in to land, the jet descending through the thin cloud-cover.

Carly packed away her papers and fastened her seatbelt. She had always been the sort of person who took every precaution she could to protect herself. But she had not been able to protect herself from what was happening to her now—and wasn't it true that a part of her didn't want to be protected from it?

'Ah, Rafael, there you are…this is Ms Carlisle.'

The young Mexican gave Carly a grave smile.

'Carly, please,' she corrected Ricardo as she shook Rafael's hand.

'Rafael and his wife Dolores run my New York apartment. How is Dolores, Rafael?'

'She is very well, and she said to tell you that she is making a special meal for you tonight. It is Italian. She also said to tell you that the orphanage is very happy and the children think you should be called Saint Salvatore.'

Saint Salvatore? Carly questioned mentally, watching the way Ricardo frowned.

'You want me to fly the chopper to the apartment block?' Rafael asked.

Ricardo shook his head.

'No, I'll fly it myself.'

Ricardo had a pilot's licence? Carly tried not to look either awed or impressed as Rafael urged her to climb on board the golf-buggy-type vehicle he had waiting for them.

She'd never flown in a helicopter before, and she acknowledged that she felt slightly daunted at the prospect of doing so. But she had no intention of saying so to Ricardo.

'I'll go and fetch the luggage,' Rafael announced, once he had helped Carly out of the buggy.

'We'll use the chopper tomorrow to get to the Hamptons,' Ricardo said as he guided Carly towards it. 'It will be much quicker and easier. You will have an excellent overview of New York City if you sit beside me. Technically Rafael should take that seat, since he is my co-pilot, but—'

'Oh, then he must sit there,' Carly insisted quickly.

'You sound apprehensive. Don't you trust me?'

'I...'

'I can assure you, I take a keen interest in my own continued existence!'

Ricardo had been right about the view of New York, Carly acknowledged, and she held her breath instinctively as he flew them between two huge tower blocks.

Via the headphones she was wearing she could hear his running commentary on the city below them—the straight lines of the modern streets, and then the curve in Broadway where the new merged with the old.

'That's Wall Street down there,' Ricardo told her, and she looked, bemused to see how quaintly narrow and small it seemed. He turned the helicopter and announced, 'We'll be flying over Central Park soon. My apartment's way up on the east side.'

The streets on either side of the park were lined with what looked like nineteenth-century buildings, and Carly held her breath as Ricardo headed for one of them, not releasing it until she saw the helicopter landing area marked out on its roof.

'You don't leave the helicopter here, do you?' Carly asked once he had helped her out.

Ricardo shook his head. 'No. Rafael will fly it back to the airport and then drive back. I dare say he will take Dolores with him, and they will call on their family on the way back.'

He was obviously a fair and well-liked employer, Carly reflected as he guided her towards the building and in through a doorway to a small foyer and lift. Once they were inside Ricardo punched a code into the panel and the doors closed, enclosing them in what—for Carly—was a far too intimate bubble of seclusion. Immediately the thought filled her mind that if he should turn to her now and take her in his arms she would not want to resist him.

'Don't look at me like that,' Ricardo warned her softly, so easily and immediately reading her thoughts that she could only gape at him. 'I can't—not in here. That's a camera up there,' he told her, pointing upwards towards the ceiling.

The lift stopped silently and smoothly and the doors opened onto another foyer. It was a large, coolly spacious one this time, with only one door opening off it, its walls painted a flat matt cream to highlight the paintings hanging on them.

'Lucien Freud?' Carly questioned, recognising the style immediately.

'Yes. His work has a raw feel to it that I like.'

The posed nudes *were* compelling, Carly admitted.

The foyer's single door opened and Ricardo stood back to allow her to precede him.

He had excellent manners, and they seemed to be a natural part of him rather than something carefully learned. But from the brief description she'd had of his early life she doubted if standing back to allow others to precede him was something he'd learned on the streets of Naples.

A small, dark-haired woman with twinkling eyes was standing in the inner hallway, waiting for them.

'Ah, Dolores. You got my message about Ms Carlisle?'

'Yes, and I have prepared a guest suite for her. You had a good journey, I hope, Ms Carlisle?'

'Yes, indeed—and do please call me Carly.'

'You go with Dolores; she will show you to your suite,' Ricardo told Carly, before continuing, 'What time is dinner planned for, Dolores?'

'Eight-thirty, if that is okay with you? And Rafael—

he said that you will want an early lunch tomorrow, before you fly to the Hamptons?'

'Yes, that's right. I'd better warn you that Ms Carlisle may not make it to the dinner table tonight. It may be three in the afternoon here, but for her it's eight in the evening.'

'Oh, my goodness! You would perhaps like something to eat now, then?' Dolores asked Carly.

'No, I'm fine,' Carly assured her.

She would have to make contact with the New York agency who were sharing the organisation of the Hamptons event with them, and she had hoped to have time to fit in a bit of sightseeing. She was also planning to ask Dolores if she could recommend somewhere Carly might find clothes that would be within her budget. Jeans might be the universal uniform, acceptable everywhere, but she could hardly turn up at the glitzy events she was overseeing wearing them. And unfortunately Mariella's cast-offs—designer label or not—were simply not the kind of clothes she would ever feel comfortable wearing.

'So, you will sleep here, in this guest suite, and you will have a lovely view over the park. Come and see, please.'

Dutifully Carly followed Dolores through the door she had just opened.

The room she walked into was huge, its windows, as Dolores had stated, overlooking the greenery of the park.

'Here there is a desk, and you can plug in your computer,' Dolores told her.

Carly nodded her head.

'And here there is a television.' She folded back what Carly had assumed was wall panelling to reveal a large flatscreen TV hidden behind it, along with shelves of DVDs and books. 'See—the TV, it pulls out so you can watch it from your bed,' Dolores told Carly, proudly displaying this extra function. 'The dressing room and your bathroom are through here. Mr Salvatore, he have everything ripped out when he moved in here, and it's all new. Even in our rooms as well.'

The dressing room was lined with mirror-fronted wardrobes and contained a small sofa, whilst the bathroom was almost a luxury mini-spa. Carly was unable to stop herself from comparing it with the rather more basic bathroom in the flat she shared with Jules.

'It's all wonderful,' she told Dolores truthfully.

'Yes. Mr Salvatore, he is a very good man. Very kind—especially to the children. When he hear that there is an orphanage in our old home town that has no money, he goes there to see it and then he writes one big cheque!' Dolores beamed.

Carly phoned Lucy and then the New York event organiser who was co-running the event. Everything seemed to be in hand, she thought as she stifled a yawn.

The bed looked very tempting, and she *was* tired. Perhaps an hour's sleep might do her good. It was only five o'clock New York time—more than three hours yet before dinner.

She was too tired to shower, and so, after removing her shoes and folding back the bedspread, she simply lay on top of the bed. Sleep claimed her the moment she closed her eyes.

CHAPTER EIGHT

IT WAS the small sound of a door clicking closed that woke her. At first she struggled to remember exactly where she was, reluctant to be dragged out of her sleeping fantasy of lying naked in Ricardo's arms whist he caressed her.

She sat up and then swung her feet onto the floor, all too aware of the pulsing ache in her lower body. She could hear someone moving about in the dressing room.

Ricardo? Her heart bumped against her ribs, excitement spiked with anticipation heating her body. If it was—if he wasn't going to give her the chance to say that she wanted him but intended instead to simply overwhelm her with the reality of her desire for him— there was no way she was going to be able to reject him, she admitted to herself, and she hurried across the room, pushing open the dressing room door.

Dolores was just closing one of the wardrobe doors. She turned towards Carly with a warm smile.

The deep-rooted sensual ache she had begun to learn to live with turned into a fierce pang of anguished need. How could just a few hours in his company have turned her body into this sexually eager collection of erotically aroused nerve endings and hotly responsive flesh? Her whole body ached, hungering for his touch and his possession. It was being consumed by a fever of longing and arousal. Virtually all she could think about was how long she would have to wait. The question driving her thoughts now wasn't 'if' but 'when'.

'I have hung everything up for you, so that they don't get too crushed. I can pack them again before you leave tomorrow. So you have any laundry you want me to do?'

Everything? What *everything*? What did Dolores mean?

There was an unfamiliar case on the dressing room floor—a Louis Vuitton case, Carly realised with horrified fascination—and a matching vanity case placed right next to it. And there was a mound of neatly folded tissue paper on the pretty daybed-cum-sofa, and some shoe boxes placed beneath it.

'Dolores, I think there must be some mistake,' she began faintly. 'Those cases aren't mine.'

Dolores looked confused.

'But, yes, they are. Rafael fetched them from the jet himself. Just as Mr Salvatore instructed him to do. So that they will not be lost.'

A horrible sense of disbelief mixed with anger was filling Carly. Unsteadily she went over to the nearest wardrobe and pulled back the door.

The clothes hanging in it were totally unfamiliar. She lifted down one of the skirts and checked the label, her hands trembling.

It was certainly her size, *and* her colour.

She put the skirt back and went over the sofa, kneeling on the floor as she opened one of the shoeboxes.

The delicate strappy sandals inside were her size too.

'There is something wrong?' Dolores asked her worriedly

Carly replaced the sandal in its box and stood up. 'No, Dolores. Everything is fine,' she told her.

But of course she was lying.

She went slowly through all the clothes hanging in

the wardrobes. Expensive, elegant, beautiful designer
clothes, in wonderful fabrics and a palette of her favourite colours: creams, chocolate-browns, black. She
touched the fringed hem of a jacket in Chanel's signature pastel tweed—warm cream threaded with tiny silky
strands of brilliant jewel colours. She had seen exactly
the same jacket in Chanel's Sloane Street store and had
stood mutely gazing at it, almost transfixed by its
beauty. It would go perfectly with the toning heavy silk
satin trousers hanging next to it. She knew exactly how
much the jacket would have cost because she had been
foolish enough to go into the store and ask. More than
she would ever spend on clothes in a whole year, never
mind on one single item. She stepped back from the
wardrobe and closed the door firmly.

Did he really think she would allow him to do this
to her? After what he had said to her? After what he
had thought of her? Oh, yes, he had claimed it was a
mistake and he had apologised, but…

Inside her head, from another lifetime, she could hear
a flustered nervous voice insisting, 'Say thank you to
the nice lady for the lovely clothes she's bought for you,
Carly. Aren't you a lucky, lucky girl? And such a very
pretty dress. I'm sure she'll be ever so grateful once she
realises how lucky she is…won't you, Carly?'

Grateful? She had sworn on her eighteenth birthday
that never, ever again was she going to have to be grateful for someone else's charity. That she would support
herself, by herself, and that was exactly what she had
done.

She had financed her own way through university via
a variety of low-paid, physically hard jobs—bar work,
cleaning, working as a nursing aide in an old people's
home—determinedly ignoring the allowance being paid

into her bank account. The first thing she had done when her adoptive parents had broken the news to her of their financial ruin had been to give that money back to them.

'Dolores, I need to speak with Ricardo. Can you tell me where I will find him, please?'

'He is in his office. But he does not like to be disturbed when he is in there.'

He didn't like being disturbed? Well, he was about to discover that neither did she. And what he had done *had* disturbed her. It had disturbed her…and it had infuriated her—a very great deal!

Dolores didn't want to give her directions for the office, but Carly insisted. She knocked briefly on the door and then, without waiting, turned the handle and went in.

Ricardo was seated behind a desk on the opposite side of the room from the door. The evening sun light coming in from the two high windows behind dazzled her whilst leaving his face cloaked in shadow.

'Dolores has filled the wardrobes in my room with clothes which she believes are mine.'

'Ah. Yes, I'm glad you reminded me; I had almost forgotten. I've spoken to the manager at Barneys and arranged a temporary account there for you so that you can get something suitable for the French do. I didn't want to risk picking out something myself. You'll have time to go over there tomorrow morning. It's right behind the Pierre Hotel—'

'No!' Carly stopped him angrily.

'No what?' Ricardo demanded, pushing back his chair and standing up.

Carly had to take a steadying breath. Every sinuous movement of his body reminded her of how it had felt against her own, of how much she wanted it, ached for it, longed for it.

Ricardo had changed his own clothes at some stage, and was wearing a tee shirt and a pair of jeans. Some men could wear jeans and some could not. Ricardo was quite definitely one of the ones who could. Longing shot through her—pure, wanton, female liquid need.

'No. I won't wear clothes that you have paid for.'

'Why not?' he demanded. 'You eat food bought with my money, sleep in a bed paid for with it. Why should you refuse to wear clothes it has bought?'

'You know why. You accused me yourself of trying to force you to—'

'I was wrong about that and I apologised.'

His voice was terse, and Carly could see he did not like being reminded that he had been at fault.

'Yes, I know that,' Carly agreed reluctantly 'But—'

'But what? You object to the colours I chose? The styles?'

'*You* chose?' she breathed in disbelief. 'How could you have done that? You couldn't possibly have had time!'

He gave a small shrug.

'I made time.'

'How?' Carly challenged him.

'I went into St Tropez this morning, before we left.'

Carly stared at him. Was he making it up…making fun of her, perhaps?

'How did you know my size?'

'I'm a man,' he told her dryly. 'I've touched your body. Held it close to my own. You have full breasts, but a very narrow ribcage. I can span your waist with my hands, your hips curve as woman's hips should do—shall I continue?'

'No,' Carly told him in a choked voice. 'I won't wear them,' she added in the next breath. 'I won't take charity.'

'Charity!' Ricardo frowned, sharply aware of the anguish in her voice, and wondering about her use of the word *charity*. 'And I will not take a woman out with me who has nothing to wear other than a pair of jeans!'

'You are not taking me out with you. I am here to work.'

'Maybe, but it is not out of the question that we could be photographed together by someone who does not know the real situation.'

'You're a snob,' Carly accused him wildly.

'No. I am a realist! I believed that you were entirely professional in your attitude towards your work, but it seems that I was wrong.'

'What do you mean?'

'I should have thought it was obvious. Were you the professional I believed you to be you would accept the necessity of dressing suitably for your role instead of behaving like an outraged virgin. Especially since we both know that is something you most definitely are *not*!'

He might think he knew that, but she knew something very different indeed, Carly reflected. 'And that is the only reason you bought the clothes?'

'What other reason could there be?' he challenged her.

'You've already made it clear to me that you think sex is something you can buy,' she pointed out. 'But I won't and can't be bought, Ricardo.'

He was very angry, she recognised, his pride no doubt stinging in much the same way as hers had when she had opened those wardrobe doors. Good!

'You're making a mountain out of a molehill. I have simply provided you with the kind of clothes I expect the women I am seen with in public to wear. That is all. Had you not had your case stolen it would not have been necessary, but it was and it is. If it makes you feel any better, then perhaps you should think of the clothes merely as being on loan to you, to wear as a necessary uniform. As for paying for sex—I think I am capable of recognising when a woman wants me, Carly.'

There was nothing she could say to that.

'It's almost dinnertime. I hope you are hungry. Dolores is very proud of her cooking,' he announced coolly, changing the subject.

Carly looked down at her jeans.

'I'm really not hungry.'

Not for food, perhaps—but for him? Ah, that was a different story. She was hungry for him—starving for him, in fact. Starving for the feel and the scent of him, for the taste of him, the reality of him. She could feel her body aching heavily with the weight of that hunger.

A sense of desolation and pain filled her. She hadn't asked to feel like this. She didn't want to feel like this. Not for any man, and least of all for a man such as this one.

Ricardo studied her downbent head. She looked tired, somehow vulnerable, and he could feel a reluctant and unwanted compassion—a desire to protect her—stirring inside him.

His only interest in her—aside from the fact that he wanted her like hell—was because of her role in Prêt a Party, Ricardo reminded himself fiercely. Emotional entanglements and complications just weren't something he had any intention of factoring into his life. He was prepared to accept that one day he might want a child—

a son, an *heir*—but when that day came he intended to satisfy that need not via marriage, with all its potential financial risks, but instead by paying a carefully selected woman to have a child for him and then to hand over all rights to it to him. With modern medical procedures he wouldn't even need to meet her.

'If you wish, I am sure Dolores will be happy to serve you dinner in your room,' he told her brusquely.

Carly veiled her eyes with her lashes, not wanting him to see what she was feeling.

If last night she had not stopped him, tonight—this night—they would have been together, and food would have been the last thing on either of their minds. It could still happen. All she had to do was go to him and touch him, show him, give way to what she was feeling. Other women had no qualms about showing men that they wanted them, so why should she?

She gave a small shiver, already knowing the answer to her own question.

CHAPTER NINE

SHE was used to the motion of the helicopter now, and did not feel as apprehensive as she had done before. They had already left New York behind them. The traffic on the highway beneath them looked like a child's toys.

She was alone with Ricardo in the helicopter this time, but he wasn't giving her a running commentary on their surroundings as he had done before. She told herself that she was glad of his businesslike attitude towards her, and the distance it had put between them.

Had he come to any decision yet as to whether or not he intended to use Prêt a Party's services? If so, she hoped that he had decided in their favour. They certainly needed the business.

She had received the e-mailed copies of the cheques she had requested and her inspection of them had confirmed what she'd already suspected. All the cheques bore—as legally they had to, according to the terms of the business—two signatures. Her own and Nick's. Only she knew that she had not signed the cheques herself. Which meant that someone had forged her signature. Someone? It could only have been Nick. Lucy was the only other person beside herself who had keys for the cupboard in which she kept the chequebooks.

Even without checking her forward costings for the year Carly knew that, because of the huge amount Nick had withdrawn from the business, by the time they reached their year-end they would be showing a loss of nearly half a million pounds.

The terms of their bank account were that Lucy would personally make up any overdraft from her trust fund. They had been in business for three years so far, and Carly had taken great pride in the fact that she had managed the financial affairs of the company so well that the bank had not had to invoke this condition. Until now.

Half a million pounds. She had no idea how much money there was in Lucy's trust fund, but she suspected that Nick would know. And she suspected too that he had made a deliberate and cold-blooded decision to help himself to money from it via the business, because he knew that Marcus would never agree to hand so much money over to him.

But understanding the situation was one thing. Knowing what to do about it was another. By rights she should tell Lucy what she had discovered, because she was sure that the *carte blanche* Lucy had given Nick to draw money from the business did not include forging Carly's signature in order to get even more. But Nick was Lucy's husband. Lucy would be bound to feel humiliated and hurt if Carly told her that he had been stealing from her. And what if Lucy refused to believe her and Nick insisted that he had not signed Carly's name? Would it be better if she got in touch with Marcus and alerted him to what was happening? Carly felt torn between her loyalty to Lucy and her fear for her.

Mentally shelving the problem, she focused instead on more immediate issues. She had spoken to her opposite number at the New York event organisers earlier, and she had assured Carly that everything was going according to plan.

'It looked like there was going to be a problem with the caterers at one stage. The magazine told us they wanted only colour-co-ordinated vegan food, in their house colours, but then they rang up saying that they'd heard that a certain glossy magazine editor only ate Beluga caviar and they had to have some.'

Carly had sympathised with her. Everyone knew how that particular British editor dictated and directed what was 'in' in certain important New York fashion circles. Just having her attend the event would be a major achievement. Of course she'd agreed gravely with her counterpart—it was essential that the caviar was provided, even though it meant breaking the colour-co-ordinated theme.

'We're serving champagne cocktails on arrival—peach and rhubarb with pepper. We're using this new chef who's into mixing together different textures and tastes. He's very *avant garde*. Virginia wants everything exclusive but statement-making simple. That's why she's chosen the Hamptons as the venue.'

Carly had continued to listen sympathetically.

Only the very richest of the rich could afford to live the 'simple' life Hamptons-style. She had read up on the area and knew that it was the preserve of those with old money—or at least it had been, until the media and fashion set had discovered it.

The magazine had been insistent that they wanted a very stylish and upmarket event—which was, Carly suspected, why they had been commissioned.

Lucy might not be the type to boast that her great-grandfather had been a duke, but the fact remained that she was very well connected socially.

'We've got the silverware on loan from Cristoffle, and the stemware is Baccarat—but very plain, of course.'

'Of course,' Carly had agreed, mentally praying that everything was well insured.

She had thought she knew what luxury was, but she had been wrong, she now admitted. As her visit to Barneys this morning had shown her. The exclusive store far surpassed anything she had ever seen, and had made her wonder who on earth could afford to shop there.

An elegant sales assistant had offered to help her, and Carly had suffered being shown a variety of stunning but impossibly expensive gowns—they could not be called anything else—before finally escaping by announcing that she had run out of time.

Any one of the dresses she had been shown would have been perfect for the French château birthday ball, but one in particular had stood out from the rest—a column of palest green silk, layer after delicately fine layer of it, the fabric floating magically with every movement of the air.

Carly had hardly dared to try it on, but the sales assistant had insisted and she had had no option other than to give way.

'It is perfect for you,' she had told Carly, and Carly had mentally agreed with her. But she had shaken her head and taken it off.

The Hamptons event was due to commence at four in the afternoon and go on until eight in the evening. A private house had been hired for the occasion, with large lawns and its own beach, and Carly had dressed—she hoped—appropriately—both for the occasion and the fact that she was part of the 'hired help', plus the fact that she was representing Lucy.

To do so she had had to give in and wear one of the outfits Ricardo had paid for. A pair of plain white Chloe linen pants teamed with an almost but not quite off the shoulder knit in navy and white. She had teamed the trousers with simple but oh, so expensive beige leather flats, and in order to accommodate all the paperwork she had to carry around with her she had splashed out this morning in New York before leaving and bought herself a large and stylish dark red straw bag—not from Barneys, where she had sighed over the unbelievable display of bags, but from a regular department store, and a marked-down sale item at that.

A couple of 'of the moment' trendy Perspex bangles, her own small gold earrings, and her good (although several years old) Oliver Peoples sunglasses completed her outfit.

She had been curious to see what Ricardo would wear. She had heard that there was an unofficial casual 'uniform' for visitors to the island—a variation on the traditional faded red jeans which had become a Hamptons visitors trademark—and had been unexpectedly touched and impressed to see that he was wearing classic Italian casual—almost as though he wanted to underline his own nationality. It was a mix of white and beige in cotton and linen, and he managed to wear it without looking either crumpled or over-groomed— which was quite an achievement.

Bare brown feet thrust into soft leather open shoes were a raw and masculine touch that certainly made her very much aware of the fact that he was dangerously male—and very much aware of him as well, she admitted, as she ignored the temptation to turn her head and look at him.

The more time she spent with him, the more she was being forced to accept how much he aroused her physically.

Even now, just sitting here beside him in silence, she could feel the tormenting ache of her own need growing stronger with every pulse of her body.

She was out of her depth. Why didn't she admit it? If he were to turn to her now and tell her that tonight he wanted to take her to bed and make love to her until morning there was no way she would refuse.

And why should she? She could go through the rest of her life without ever again meeting a man who could make her feel like this.

And sex without love was surely like… Like what? Like whisky without water? Undiminished? Its strength and flavour heightened by the fact that it was not touched by anything else? Why shouldn't sex be like that? Why shouldn't it? Why couldn't it be a pure, intense, once-in-a-lifetime experience just as it was?

What she had to ask herself was, if she didn't have sex with Ricardo, in later years would she praise herself or would she berate herself? Would she feel that she had gained or lost? Would she yearn to have the opportunity back again or…?

What was she trying to do? Persuade herself into bed with him? Wasn't that Ricardo's role? Nothing about him suggested to her that he was the kind of man who wasn't capable of going in all-out pursuit of anything and everything he wanted, be it a woman or a business. Ricardo played to win. If he truly wanted her he would be the one doing the persuading—and he would surely have persuaded her into his bed by now! As if she actually needed persuading, she admitted wryly.

But why did she want him so much? It definitely wasn't because of his money! And equally definitely it wasn't because of love. Loving someone meant risking being hurt.

So it was the man himself, then? The tightening sensation within her own body told her she had found the truth.

All these years of believing she wasn't interested in sex—she had told herself that nothing would ever induce her to adopt the casual attitude towards sex of so many women she knew, which she found repugnant—had been washed away by the ferocity of her own desire, like a dam bursting its banks to flood a hitherto dried-out gully.

She had a terrible and terrifying urge to turn to Ricardo and ask him to turn the helicopter around. To take her back to New York and his apartment, his bed, so that she could discover for herself which was the more powerfully sensual and erotic—her fantasies or Ricardo's reality.

When had the balance, the scales themselves tipped? Ricardo wondered savagely as he tried to fight against the message his body's fierce hunger was sending him.

When had his hunger for Carly started to occupy his thoughts more than acquiring Prêt a Party? When had he somehow given way and abandoned the rule he'd thought he had set in stone never to allow himself to want any woman so much that the wanting overpowered him?

He didn't know! What he did know, though, was that he had looked at her earlier, when she had walked towards him in his apartment, and had had to fight against the madness of an overwhelming need to take hold of her and kiss her until he could feel in her the same passionate response he had felt in her before—until her body was pliant and eagerly, erotically desirous of his touch, and her breathing was signalling an arousal that matched his own.

They had almost reached their destination; he could see the helipad up ahead of him. It was too late to turn back now.

East Hampton. New money and lots of it—or at least that was what she had read, Carly thought as a uniformed hunk, wearing eye-wateringly canary-yellow cut-offs and a bright blue logoed polo shirt—all muscles and too-white teeth—tenderly handed her down from the helicopter. What was it about such movie-perfect men that was so antiseptic and unsexy? Carly mused as she was asked for her name. And was it her imagination or did the bright smile fade just a little once its owner realised she was here as part of the workforce?

To the side of her, though, Ricardo was being greeted almost effusively by a stunningly pretty girl also wearing a greeter's uniform.

So this was corporate entertaining New York style! Certainly everything was well organised, very slick and professional—right down to the small packs they were being handed which she already knew included a map of the layout of the house and its gardens, a timetable of the afternoon's events, and a ticketed voucher so that guests could collect their goodie bags as they left—no cluttering the tables or, even worse, disgruntled guests leaving rejected and unwanted gifts behind them.

Ricardo was certainly receiving the *de luxe* treatment,

Carly decided, as a further glance in his direction informed her that his greeter was still making him the focus of her attention whilst her own had mysteriously disappeared. He was nursing a half-empty glass of red wine, glancing away from his companion to stare down into its depths.

If Ricardo were a glass of full-bodied, richly flavoured red wine, Carly thought fancifully, she would want to drink deeply of him, not sip delicately at him. She would want to roll the glorious velvety texture of him around her tongue before allowing him to turn the whole of her body to liquid pleasure. She would want to breathe in the richness of him and savour his unique musky flavour. She would want to fill her senses with the richness of him and then...

Hot-faced, Carly struggled to call her thoughts to order. Ricardo wasn't a wine, he was a man. And just seeing the way he was smiling back at the girl who was so obviously flirting with him filled Carly with a fierce, painful surge of jealousy.

She was here to work, she reminded herself starkly, and she turned her back on Ricardo and made her way towards the main hospitality area.

They were, of course, virtually the first arrivals, and Carly wanted to check in with both the New York event organiser and the clients to make sure that everything was going to plan. Waiters and waitresses—their uniforms comprising retro Hawaiian-style shirts with a brilliantly patterned design made up of front covers of the magazine—were already circulating with trays of drinks, presumably serving the clients themselves.

When Carly reached the main pavilion a security guard on the door stopped her, and she showed him both her pass and her identity badge. Once inside, she found the magazine's PR team and Luella Klein, her opposite number from the New York event organiser, standing together, engaged in conversation.

'*Lurve* the shirts those guys out there are wearing!' Luella announced dramatically as soon as the introductions were over.

'That was Jules's idea.' Carly smiled.

'Yeah, great—and cool, too. We've had the goodie bags made out of the same fabric!'

Carly nodded her head. Using the magazine's past covers as a basis for the design theme of the event had been the result of a brainstorming session held between Lucy, Jules and herself when they had first been approached to pitch for this event.

Getting a canapé menu organised that would translate into plates of food put together in the magazine's house colours had proved to be a major headache, though, with several chefs refusing the commission before Carly had had the bright idea of getting one of the top catering colleges to take it on as a showcase for the talents of their students.

She was just keeping her fingers crossed that the results would be as impressive as the sample plates they had seen photographs of earlier in the year.

'And it may sound kinda silly, but I've always had a thing about Italian men—'

'I'm sorry—I have to go.'

The young woman, who had spent the best part of the last fifteen minutes congratulating herself on having got Ricardo's exclusive attention, just about managed not to stamp her expensive heel down into the turf as he cut through her breathless words and started to walk away. Her chagrin gave way to resentment as she saw that he had left her to go to someone else—a woman who was standing with a group of caterers, of all things. Grudgingly she acknowledged that the white linen trousers her competitor was wearing did do full justice to legs that, as the male sex would have it, went all the way up to her armpits.

Carly smiled her thanks at the team leaders of the hired catering staff. It was nearly nine in the evening and most of the guests had left. Most, but not all. Not, for instance, the baby blonde whom she had seen clinging fragilely to Ricardo's arm earlier in the afternoon, whilst she had been talking to a trio of famous British fashionista sisters whom she knew, in a roundabout sort of way, via mutual contacts in London.

The clients had just told her how pleased they were with the event, and her New York opposite number had said that she knew her agency would want to do business with Prêt a Party again.

All in all, a successful event. A successful event but not, so far she was concerned, a personally successful or mood-enhancing few hours. But then she was not here for her own benefit, was she? Carly reminded herself, as she dismissed the waiting staff and wondered how long it would be before she could reasonably suggest to Ricardo that they leave.

Two men—executives from a big New York PR agency to whom she had been introduced earlier—were approaching her. She forced her lips to widen in what she hoped looked like a genuine professional smile.

'Good event,' one of them told her approvingly. 'Harvey thought it was real neat—didn't you, Harv?'

'Yeah,' the second one agreed. 'Real neat!'

Ricardo increased the pace of his stride. Every time he gave in to his need to look for her Carly was surrounded by other men. And he didn't like it. He didn't like it one little bit!

'Sorry to break up the party,' he announced untruthfully now, as he reached the trio.

Immediately the two men fell back, leaving an empty space at Carly's side, which Ricardo promptly filled. As he did so he deliberately stood so that he was blocking out the other men—and anyone else who might have wanted to approach Carly.

'Have you seen everything you want to see?' Carly asked him brightly. All afternoon she had been reminding herself that she was supposed to be making sure that Ricardo was so impressed with Prêt a Party's skills that he offered them a contract.

Ricardo was tempted to tell her bluntly and in explicit detail that *she* was what he most wanted to see—preferably lying naked on his bed, with that look in her eyes that said she wanted him like crazy.

Instead he nodded his head tersely and asked, 'How soon can you be ready to leave?'

Her New York counterpart had already assured her that there was no need for her to stay, and she had spoken with the clients.

'I'm ready now.'

'Fine. Let's go, then.'

Carly didn't really want to move. Ricardo was standing right next to her, and if she turned towards him now they would be standing body to body...like lovers...

'What's wrong? Missing the attention of your new friends? Want me to call them back?'

Instead of turning towards him, Carly took a step back.

'No, I don't,' she told him quietly. 'And as for what's

wrong—I was just wishing that I didn't ache so much for you to take me to bed!'

She turned away from him and started to walk towards the helipad, trembling inside from the shock of actually having told him what she was thinking and how she felt. Her face and body both felt equally hot, but for very different reasons. Her face was burning because of her embarrassment, but her body was burning because what she had said to him was the truth.

Ricardo caught up with her before she had taken more than three steps, his hand on her arm halting her progress until he could stand four-square in front of her.

'Is that an admission or is it an invitation?' he asked silkily.

Carly forced herself to look up at him, and to hold his gaze as she responded calmly, 'Both!'

Ricardo couldn't even remember how many women had propositioned him over the years, never mind count them, but none of them had ever spoken to him like this—simply and directly, admitting and owning their need for him.

'That's quite a change of heart! Why?'

'I suddenly realised how much I would regret it if I went to my grave without knowing you.'

'*Knowing* me?'

His voice was cynically mocking as he moved aside so that they could continue to walk together to the helipad.

'Without having sex with you,' Carly corrected herself steadily. 'Obviously it goes without saying that it *is* only sex that we both want.'

'Less than twenty-four hours ago you were outraged because I'd paid for your clothes. Now you're offering to have sex with me?'

'I was furious because I felt what you'd done implied that I could be bought. Choosing freely to have sex with you is completely different.'

'Indeed. Didn't it occur to you that I might feel equally insulted by your suggestion that I would want a woman I had to bribe into bed with me?' he challenged her.

They had almost reached the helipad.

She had spoken to him, touched a deeply secret part of him, as no other woman had ever done, and instinctively he felt wary of his own emotional response to that. At the same time he also felt challenged by the fact that she was so obviously determined not to allow herself to become emotionally involved with him. A woman who wanted to give herself freely to him physically whilst refusing to become emotionally involved? Shouldn't that knowledge delight him instead of irking him? he taunted himself derisively. He certainly wasn't going to refuse her, was he?

Carly wondered what he was thinking. Was Ricardo shocked by what she had said? Turned off by it? Indifferent to it? Should she have been less direct, and instead created an artificial opportunity for him to come on to her if he wanted to do so?

Ricardo had gone to speak to the ground staff brought in to take care of the helicopters lined up away from the helipad. She could feel her stomach muscles clench as he walked back to her.

'I was watching you earlier on today,' he told her softly. 'Imagining just what it would be like to have those long legs of yours wrapped tightly around me whilst I took you. How do you like it best? Tell me!'

Shocked pleasure rushed through her, hot, sweet and

intoxicating. A dizzying, breathtaking sensation of open and responsive arousal.

Ricardo watched her, acknowledging that the look of dazzled, dazed anticipation in her eyes was doing more to arouse him than he would have thought possible.

'Time to go,' he said, nodding in the direction of the waiting helicopter.

'You've been very quiet. Second thoughts?' Ricardo challenged Carly as he piloted them towards the landing pad of his New York building.

'About what? Telling you that I want you? Or the fact that I do want you?'

Did she realise how the musical sound of her voice could play on a man's desire, heightening it and arousing him? Ricardo wondered as he looked directly at her.

'Either.'

Carly shook her head. She had spent most of the flight surreptitiously sneaking glances at Ricardo and then imagining herself touching him, learning him, allowing the fantasy that she hoped would soon become a reality to guide and slightly shock her thoughts. She'd touch first with her fingertips, tracing the bones that shaped him, and then with her hands as she absorbed the strength of his muscles and the taut smoothness of his flesh. And then finally with her lips and her tongue, as she explored every delicate hollow and plane of him.

The heat that constantly beat through her body was roaring now, pulse-points of urgency throbbing not just between her legs and in her breasts but everywhere— her fingertips, her toes, her lips—everywhere…

'I've said more than I should,' she admitted huskily.

'Yes,' Ricardo acknowledged coolly. 'You have.

Haven't the other men in your life preferred to do their own hunting and their own propositioning?'

There was a small jolt as the helicopter hit the ground.

She waited silently for Ricardo to climb out and then come round to help her. Above them, stars glittered in the darkness of the night sky, but it was impossible for them to compete with the brilliance and colour of the New York skyline.

His hands on her body felt hard but remote. Rejecting? Had she got it wrong? Had she misunderstood? Had he merely been pretending before that he wanted her?

He had set her free, and she had no option other than to walk ahead of him to the lift foyer door.

Ricardo followed her and activated the lift. Within seconds they were stepping out of it into his own private entrance foyer, and within seconds of that he was opening the door to his apartment.

'Dolores and Rafael are away for a family event,' he told her.

Carly nodded her head. Disappointment was a cold, sick, leaden lump weighing down her body. It struck her how ironic it was. Had someone previously suggested to her that she would find herself in this kind of situation, the feelings she would have expected would have been shame and humiliation, rather than the gut-wrenching sense of disappointment she actually did have.

All those years of silently, determinedly telling herself she had a right to her pride had obviously not made as big an impression on her psyche as she had believed.

They were in the large square hallway. It was nearly eleven o'clock. She turned away from Ricardo, intending to make her way to her suite and the sleepless night she suspected lay ahead of her.

'This way.'

His fingers closed round her bare forearm and immediately her flesh reacted in a burst of over-sensitivity and raised goosebumps.

This corridor was unfamiliar, its walls hung with what she suspected must be priceless pieces of modern art. At the end of it was a pair of double doors. Ricardo opened one of them without releasing her.

Silently she walked through it into the darkness that lay beyond. Ricardo let her go, and she heard the quiet snap of the door closing.

She could feel him standing behind her, and waited for him to switch on the lights, but instead he turned her round, his hands gripping her upper arms.

CHAPTER TEN

'Now. *Now* you can tell me that you want me.'

His voice was a raw sound of out-of-control male need.

A thrill of shocked delight exploded inside her. She could feel herself shaking with excitement as he pulled her into his own body and took her mouth with explicit sexual hunger.

Her response to him rolled over her like an eighty-foot wave, swamping her, picking her up and taking her bodily. She had no defence against it, nor did she want one.

His tongue, seeking and demanding, thrust hotly between her lips without any preliminaries. Her small sob of pleasure was submerged beneath his own sounds of overriding need. His hands were on her body, tugging down her top, pushing aside her bra.

Carly moaned as his hands grazed her nipples, and then moaned again more sharply when he took one between his thumb and forefinger and began to tease it into hard, tight, aching need. Without knowing she was doing it Carly ground her hips against him, mimicking the hard thrust of his tongue between her lips.

'Don't,' he cautioned her thickly. 'Do you want me to completely lose control and take you here?'

Getting her back here without touching her had strained his self control to its limits. And now…

'Yes,' Carly told him quickly, feeling the words catch against her throat. 'I want you to take me, wherever and whenever you want—but most of all I want you to do it *now*. Now! Ricardo, now!'

Did she realise that she had just destroyed the last shreds of his control, what her hungry, half-moaned words were doing to him?

'Now?' he repeated.

His eyes, accustomed to the darkness, showed him the pale glimmer of her breasts. He stroked his forefinger round one nipple and watched her whole body surge with pleasure. He could feel the muscles locking in his throat. He bent his head and took the tight sexual flowering of her desire for him into his mouth, savouring the sensation of the smooth swell of her breast before running his tongue over her nipple, all the time trying to hold onto his sanity, to stop himself from pushing her up against the wall and tearing the clothes off her so that he could have the pleasure of sinking as deep inside her as he could get.

Carly could hear someone start to moan, but it took her several seconds to recognise that she was the one making the noise. She felt as though she were on a long slide, unable to stop herself from plunging into her own pleasure. Not wanting to stop herself.

Reluctantly Ricardo released her nipple, his fingers immediately returning to enjoy its arousal.

'How do you want it?' he demanded softly. 'Do you have a favourite position? Do you want to take care of the condom issue or shall I?'

Carly looked at him and took a deep breath. 'I think this is when I should tell that I don't have very much previous experience,' she announced carefully.

'What?'

She couldn't tell whether the harshness in his voice came from anger or disbelief.

'What does that mean?'

Carly swallowed, and then said in a small voice,

'Actually, I'm afraid it means that I haven't… There hasn't… I'm still a virgin.'

'*What?* You're joking, right?'

Carly shook her head.

He released her abruptly and stood back from her, looking at her for what felt like for ever.

'I can't think of one single reason why the hell you would be a virgin.'

'Actually, there are several,' Carly responded with dignity. 'For one thing… Well, I don't suppose the opportunity has been there at the right time or with the right man,' she hedged.

Her revelation was the last thing Ricardo had expected. If she had kept to her virgin purity until now why was she, to put it crudely, offering it to him on a plate? Did she think he would feel some sort of moral responsibility towards her? Was that it? Was she setting some sort of trap for him? Would she try to use emotional blackmail to turn mere physical intimacy into something more?

If he had any sense he would send her back to her own room, right now, but somehow, in some way, a part of him was actually responding to what she had told him with a primitive surge of male possessiveness. It actively *liked* the thought of the sexual exclusivity of being her first lover, of knowing that the sensuality he would imprint on her would remain with her throughout her life, that if the experience he gave her was truly pleasurable then she would treasure it all her life. And she would not be comparing him to anyone else. Was he really that vain? That insecure? Ricardo grimaced to himself, knowing that he wasn't.

'You damn sure don't act like a virgin,' he told her grimly.

Probably because when she was around him she didn't think that she was. Mentally, in the privacy of her own thoughts, the intimacy she had with him had gone well beyond the bounds of virginity.

'Perhaps I shouldn't have told you?' Carly offered.

Ricardo looked at her with incredulity.

'Don't you think it would have been obvious? Especially given the kind of intimacy I'd planned to—'

He saw the excitement begin to burn in her eyes and he cursed himself for the way his body immediately responded to it.

'Are you sure this is what you want? An affair that—?'

Carly stopped him. 'I don't want an affair. I just want to have sex with you.'

'Just sex?' Ricardo questioned, not sure that he believed her.

'Yes. But of course if you'd rather not…' she added lightly.

No one gave that kind of challenge to Ricardo.

'You'll cry "enough" before I do,' he told her against her mouth.

He was barely brushing her lips with his own, a feather-light touch that, as Carly quickly discovered, made her hunger for more. Her own lips clung to his, willing him to part them with his tongue as he had done before, and a shudder of visible pleasure gripped her body when finally he did so, thrusting the seeking point of his tongue deep and hard within the warm softness of her mouth.

His hand cupped the back of her head and his tongue plunged deeper, twining with her own. She could feel the heavy slam of her heart as it banged against her ribs—or was it his?

He was holding her right up against him, so close that she could feel his erection. And she wanted to feel it. And not just to feel it—she wanted to see it, touch it…experience it deep inside her.

She felt weak and dizzy with arousal, her whole body shuddering with pleasure when Ricardo cupped her breast and then slowly circled his fingertip around her nipple. Lazy delicate circles that were driving her insane. She sucked in a deep breath and felt the corresponding tightening low down in her body. Unable to stop herself, she reached out and touched the hard ridge of male flesh, mimicking Ricardo's caress as she circled the head of it with her fingertip and then traced its whole shape through the fabric of his clothes. It felt thick and strong. Her fingers trembled and so did her body.

To her shock Ricardo immediately released her. She stared up at him through the darkness.

'I need a shower,' he told her thickly, 'and you are going to share it with me.'

He had taken hold of her hand. She could break free of him if she wanted to, but she knew that she didn't.

He guided her through the darkness past the shape of a huge bed and then into a dressing room, switching on the light as he did so.

'It's a wet room,' he told her. 'So we undress in here.'

Undress. Her mouth went dry. But Ricardo had turned away from her and was already stripping off his clothes.

Mesmerised, Carly watched him, her curiosity followed by an awe that darkened her eyes so that when

Ricardo looked at her he could see arousal shimmering in them, just as she could see his arousal, straining tautly from its thick mat of dark springy curls.

Her legs had suddenly gone weak.

Her fingers trembling, she started to tug off her own clothes, hesitating only when she got down to the silky sheer thong that barely concealed her sex.

Ricardo had turned away from her and was walking towards the door to the wet room. Carly took a deep breath and then followed him.

Ricardo touched a button, and immediately lusciously warm water sprang from hidden jets, soaking her.

'Do you really need this?' Ricardo was standing in front of her, hooking one lean finger under the narrow strap of her thong whilst the pad of his thumb stroked sensuously against her bare skin. Thrills of pleasure skittered over her.

He leaned forward and stroked his tongue-tip over her lips. Carly exhaled in a voluptuous sigh and closed her eyes, moving closer to him. The soft stroking touch of his fingertip traced the edge of her thong very slowly, and then traced it again.

'Mmm…'

She could feel the heat building up between her legs.

Ricardo's fingertip was tracing down the side of her thong. She could feel herself starting to shudder.

His hand moved back, easing her thong down…out of his way. Her legs had gone so weak she could barely stand to step out of it.

Half dazed, she started to soap herself, tensing when Ricardo took hold of her hands and told her softly, 'That's my job—and my pleasure.'

The silky suds made his hands glide sensuously over her flesh: her breasts, exquisitely sensitive now to his touch, her belly, where the spread of his fingers caused the heat inside her to turn her liquid with longing, her behind, which he soaped with a long slow movement that left one hand resting on the back of her thigh whilst the fingers of the other stroked between her legs, and then right up along the wet cleft between the swollen lips of her sex.

Helplessly Carly leaned into his caress, her body clenching on shudders of arousal. Driven by age-old instinct, she reached out and enclosed him with her hand, eagerly caressing the full length of him, and then released him again so that she could explore the swollen head of his erection. Now he was the one doing the shuddering, then subjecting them both to a sudden swift pounding of more water jets to rinse their bodies free of suds.

She had always believed that she was far too tall and heavy for any man to ever be able to pick her up bodily, but now, for a second time, Ricardo was proving her wrong, Carly thought, as Ricardo finished towelling her dry and then lifted her into his arms.

The bedroom was now bathed in soft lamplight, and the bedlinen was cool beneath her skin as Ricardo laid her on the bed and then bent his head towards her own.

'Still want this?' he whispered against her lips.

'Yes,' Carly whispered back. 'Do you?'

For the first time since she had known him she saw genuine humour in his eyes.

'My arousal and desire are quite plainly evident.'

'So are mine—to me,' Carly told him huskily.

His hand cupped her breast. 'You mean this—here?' he murmured, his thumb stroking lightly against her nipple. 'Or this—here?' His knowing stroke the full length of her sex made her moan with pleasure. Her arousal-swollen flesh housed a million nerve endings that were pleasure points, and it seemed to Carly that Ricardo's caress lingered over each one of them. And then he stroked her clitoris, rhythmically and deliberately.

Immediately her body arched in supplication, her gaze fixed on his. How could she ever have thought his eyes were cold? They burned now with dark fire.

His hand moved away. He kissed the side of her throat and then her collarbone, sliding his free hand into her hair and cradling the back of her head. Already she was anticipating—longing for the feel of his mouth against her.

Her throat tightened, shudders of pleasure running through her as his tongue-tip traced a lazy line down to her breasts and circled each nipple. A soft breath of longing bubbled in her throat. His lips closed over one nipple, his tongue working it. She gasped breathlessly, reaching out to hold his head against her body, her fingers locking into his hair as she arched up against him, unable to stop herself from wanting the wild surges of pleasure his mouth and fingers were creating inside her.

Of their own volition her legs fell open, her muscles contracting as she felt the warmth of Ricardo's hand skimming her body and then coming to rest against the small curls covering her sex.

Heat ran through her to gather beneath his hand. A pulse of need was beating where he touched her.

She had believed that she knew desire, but all she had known was its shadow. This, its reality, was overpowering, overwhelming her.

She felt Ricardo's thumb probing the cleft below the soft curls. A pleading, mewling sound broke from her lips and she lifted her body towards him.

The dark fire in his eyes burned even more hotly. But not as hot as the fire burning inside her.

Wild tremors seized her and she whimpered in helpless arousal as he parted the outer lips of her sex and then started to caress her.

The white heat of ravening need filled her, her head falling back against the pillows. Her hips writhed frantically against the movement of his fingertip as he rubbed it the full length of her, lingering deliberately on the hard swell of her clitoris.

No woman had ever abandoned herself, given herself to him and his pleasuring of her like this, Ricardo acknowledged. He didn't know how much longer he could keep his own arousal under control.

She felt hot and wet, the swollen lips beneath his fingers opening to him of their own volition to offer him the gift of her sex.

A wild surge of longing engulfed him. It wasn't enough that he could feel her; he wanted to see her as well.

Carly cried out in protest as she felt Ricardo move, but his hand was still resting reassuringly on the mound of her sex and his body was still openly aroused. Her eyes, though, still asked an anxious question, and as he sat up Ricardo answered it for her, telling her rawly, 'I want to see you. I want to watch your sex flush with pleasure and lie open and eager for my touch.'

Wild thoughts of urging him, begging him not to, fled, as she felt him caressing her again. But this time… This time, as her head dropped back and her body was gripped by intense surges of pleasure, she could feel him caressing her lips apart, exposing her swollen, glistening secret inner flesh to his gaze and his touch. Just the pressure of his fingertip against her clitoris made her cry out in frantic arousal. He bent his head and his tongue stroked along her silken folds. All the way along them, Carly recognised on a shudder of fierce delight, as the hard-pointed tip of his tongue probed and stroked into life sensations she had never imagined existing.

He couldn't hold out much longer, Ricardo realised, as he felt his body throb in reaction to the pleasure of tasting her and arousing her. He drove the tip of his tongue into her moist opening and heard her moan of pleasure He stroked her clitoris with quick rhythmic strokes of his tongue and eased a finger slowly into her.

Immediately her muscles closed round it, holding it, and his body responded with a savage thrust of male urgency.

He could feel his heart thudding, sweat beading his forehead, but he made himself go slowly. One finger, and then two, waiting for her body to accommodate him and then respond as he caressed her.

She was moving urgently against him now, her body aroused and eager as she thrust against him and moaned.

Frantically Carly reached out and touched Ricardo's body, her fingers closing round him, moving over him. He felt so hot and slick, the foreskin moving easily and fluidly over the swollen head of his erection. Her body tightened, and excitement locked the air into her lungs in expectation.

Still caressing her, Ricardo pulled her beneath him, easing himself slowly into her, his muscles aching with the punishing pressure he was exerting over them as he refused to give in to their demand for him to thrust deeply and fully.

Her muscles closed round him, making him shudder with violent need. He thrust deeper, and then deeper still, whilst Carly dug her nails into his shoulder—not in pain, but in urgent female need to have more of him. Unable to stop herself, she gave voice to that need, the words tumbling huskily from her lips as she pleaded frantically, 'More... Ricardo. Deeper...' matching her pleas to the eager movement of her body against his.

'Like this? How much more? This much?'

She gasped into his thrust, driven by her own need to make him fill her and take her higher.

'Mmm. Yes. More...deeper...again.'

Her frantic litany of pleas and praise fell against Ricardo's senses like a song sung in sensual counterpart to their mingled breathing, underscored by the rise and fall of its urgency and satisfaction, whilst her body's response to him blew apart his intention of remaining in control.

His own need to go deeper, harder, to know and possess all of her, overwhelmed him. His increasingly powerful thrusts took them both higher, and his own satisfaction was matched by the eager rhythmic movement of Carly's hips, and the sounds of her rising pleasure. She clung to him, kissing his throat and his shoulder, then raking his arm with her nails in a sudden ecstasy of physical delight as he drove them both closer to the edge.

It was too much for his self-control. The muscles in his neck corded as he fought to delay his own climax, but it was too late. His body was already claiming its final mindless driving surge of release.

Carly called out a jumble of helpless words of feverish pleasure as Ricardo's fierce pulsing thrusts of completion carried her with him over the edge of pleasure, her body suddenly contorting in a burst of rhythmic climactic contractions of release.

It was over.

Very carefully, Ricardo rolled Carly over onto her side and held her against him.

Carly lay there, trying to steady her breathing, her body still trembling with reaction. Tears blurred her vision, although she had no idea why she should want to cry. The pleasure had been so very much more than she had imagined.

Ricardo was lying facing her, his arm resting heavily but oh, so sweetly over her, holding her close to him.

'Are you okay?'

'I think so,' she answered shakily. 'I'm still trying to come back down to earth. I hadn't realised it would be so...' She stopped.

'So what?' Ricardo probed.

'So...so intense. Not when you ...when we don't... when this isn't about loving one another,' she finally managed to say.

She felt Ricardo moving, but before she could say anything he was holding her tightly in his arms and kissing her. Slowly and gently and...oh, so very sweetly.

It was six o'clock and the park was quiet. Ricardo had left Carly sleeping, easing himself away from her body and taking care not to wake her.

He had woken a dozen times during the night, silently listening to her breathing, watching her, and whilst he was doing so he had relived the intimacy they had shared, trying to analyse his own reaction to it.

He had had sex before, after all, and he had had good sex before. But never, ever anything that had come anywhere near to making him feel the way he had felt with Carly.

Her use of the word 'intense' had mirrored his own feelings.

Why, though? Why should her body, her flesh, her need be so very different? Not because she had been a virgin? No, definitely not because of that!

The second time they had made love, in the early hours of the morning, had to him been an even more intense experience than the first time. And Carly had made it plain to him that she had no regrets. Her virginity had been something he'd had to take account of in possessing her, yes, but it had not been the cause of that difference.

So what was it about her that lingered so strongly that he had needed to keep waking up to check that she was still there?

What was it about her that made his whole body compress with possessiveness at the thought of losing her?

Was it the intensity of the intimacy they had shared? The fact that, for some unfathomable reason, something in her humbled and softened something in him? He didn't know. But he did know that, whatever it was, it had somehow caused an abrupt turnaround inside his head, and that instead of mentally working out how fast he could get away from her and get on with the really exciting things in his life—like another business acquisition—he was actually wondering how he could prolong their time together.

He looked at his watch. Soon she would be waking up. And he wanted to be there when she did.

'Carly?'

Reluctantly she opened her eyes.

She had woken up an hour earlier, wondering where Ricardo had gone, and then, after showering and brushing her teeth, she had come back to bed and promptly fallen deeply asleep again.

Ricardo was sitting on the side of the bed next to her, and what was more he was fully dressed.

She struggled to sit up, and then realised self-consciously that she was naked.

'We need to leave for France this afternoon,' Ricardo reminded her.

'Oh, yes, of course. I—'

She gave a shallow gasp as Ricardo leaned forward and covered her mouth with his own. Automatically she clung to his shoulders, and then wrapped her arms around his neck when she felt his tongue demanding possession of her mouth. Already her body felt sweetly heavy with longing for him, drawn to him like a moth to a flame.

He lifted his mouth from hers and she stretched sensuously, watching the heat burn in his gaze as it feasted on her, relishing the hot glitter. His hand cupped her shoulder and then stroked slowly over her, ignoring the urgent, desiring peaking of her nipples and coming to rest on her hip, his thumb moving lazily over the indent of her belly. Feathery, frustrating little touches that had her arching up to him in silent demand.

'Undress me!'

The command sounded thick and slightly unsteady, rather like her own fingers as they curled round the hem of his tee shirt and then trembled wildly the minute they came into contact with the hard-muscled heat of his skin.

Her task might have been easier if Ricardo hadn't tormented her, occupying himself by kissing her and caressing her whilst she was trying to complete it, Carly decided, but she finally tugged off his tee shirt, to be rewarded with the hot fierce suckle of his mouth on her breast.

Sensation pierced her, sweet and shocking and achingly erotic, and the stroke of his tongue and the deliberate, delicate rasp of his teeth made her moan and beg for more.

In the end he had to finish undressing himself, shedding his clothes with unsteady urgency and then taking hold of Carly and lifting her to straddle his prone body.

He watched as her eyes widened, and kept on watching whilst he stroked his fingertip through her wetness.

She cried out immediately, her body tensing. Ricardo reached up and laved first one and then the other nipple with his tongue, feral male arousal gripping him as the morning sun highlighted for him the swollen wet crests. He found the sensitive heat of her clitoris and rubbed his fingertip rhythmically over it.

Carly arched tightly against his touch, her eagerness for him darkening her eyes as she reached for him and positioned herself over him, slowly sinking down on him, taking him into her.

Ricardo kept still, hardly daring to breathe, hardly able to endure the pleasure of the sensation of her body opening to him, her muscles slowly claiming him.

Experimentally Carly moved her body, gasping in shocked delight as she felt her own pleasure. She moved again, eagerly and demandingly. Exhaling, Ricardo responded to her need, grasping her hips as she took control, letting her take as much of him as she wanted, and then groaning in raw heat as she demanded more.

She came quickly, almost violently, just before Ricardo, in a series of intense spasms that left her too weak to even move. It was left to Ricardo to lift her from him and then hold her sweat-slick trembling body against his own, his arms wrapped securely around her.

CHAPTER ELEVEN

'I SHOULD really stay at the château, so that I can be on hand in case anything goes wrong.'

They had arrived in France two hours ago, and now Carly was seated next to Ricardo in the large Mercedes hire car that had been waiting for him at the airport. He had just informed her that he wanted her to stay with him at the house he was renting instead of at the château where the party was to be held.

'If anything does go wrong you can be there within minutes,' he told her.

She knew that he was right, and she knew too that she wanted to be with him. How, in such a short space of time, could she have become so physically addicted to him that she could hardly bear not to be close to him?

'How are you feeling? Are you okay?'

Both his question and the almost tender note in his voice startled her.

'I'm—I'm fine. I can't believe I didn't realise before how...how compulsive sex can be.'

Ricardo started to frown. Her answer wasn't the one he had been expecting. Or the one he had wanted?

'It wasn't just sex for you, though, was it?' he challenged her.

Carly couldn't look at him. Prickles of warning were burning their way into her head, triggering her defences.

'Why do you say that?'

'A woman doesn't get to your age still a virgin unless

she's either too traumatised to want sex or she's waiting to feel as drawn to a partner emotionally as she is sexually.'

'No, that isn't true. The reason I haven't had sex before now is because I *haven't* wanted any emotional involvement, not because I have.'

Ricardo could hear the panic in her voice. No matter how old-fashioned it might be, every instinct he possessed told him that she had to have very deep emotional feelings for him to have responded the way she had. His male logic couldn't accept that, given her virginity, it could be any other way.

'Human beings are allowed to have emotions, you know,' he told her wryly. 'But my guess is that you are afraid of emotional vulnerability because of what you experienced as a child. Your adoptive parents rejected you, gave their love to their own daughter whilst withholding it from you.'

Carly was too intelligent to try and deny what he was saying.

'I may have been an emotionally needy child, but I have no intention of allowing myself to become an emotionally needy woman.'

'There's a huge difference between being emotionally needy and loving someone.'

'Maybe. Or maybe, just as some people are genetically disposed to be more vulnerable to drug addiction, some people might be genetically disposed to emotional vulnerability. I prefer not to put my own resistance to the test.'

'How did your adopted sister die?'

His question caught her off guard.

'She…she was a drug addict. She died from an overdose of heroin. She started using drugs when we were at school. She was a year above me, and in a different crowd. I… It never appealed to me. I told you that my mother was one of three young women who died in a house fire. They were probably all drug addicts. I never… I couldn't… I know that, deep down inside, my adoptive parents blamed me for her addiction. My adoptive mother admitted as much. She said that she felt by bringing me into their lives they had brought in the evil of drug addiction.'

'Rubbish,' Ricardo announced briskly. 'It strikes me that they were looking for someone to blame and picked on you.'

'Maybe, but I still feel guilty. They loved her, not me, and now she's dead. All they've got left is me. I've tried to do what I can to help them, to repay them for everything they've given me.'

'Everything they've given you? Such as what?'

'A chance to live a normal life. My education. Without them I could have ended up making a living selling myself on the street, like my mother probably did.'

'No,' Ricardo told her firmly. 'No, you would never have done that. Somehow you would have found a way to set yourself free.'

Carly could feel emotional tears prickling her eyes. Emotional tears?

'I want you, Carly, and not just physically. You touch my emotions and delight my senses. When you aren't with me, I want you to be. You've become integral to my pleasure in life—to my happiness, if you like. I want to explore with you what's happening to us. I trust you enough to tell you that, and to tell you too that emotionally I am vulnerable to you. Is it really so hard for you to do the same?'

'I don't know what to say,' she admitted shakily.

'Then don't say anything,' Ricardo told her. 'Just allow yourself to feel instead. And when we're together you *do* feel, don't you, Carly?'

'I…I know that when we have sex it gives me a lot of pleasure.'

She answered him primly, but prim was the very opposite of what she felt. Just talking with him like this had made her body begin to pulse with sensual need. It seemed a lifetime since they had last had sex, though in fact it was less than twenty-four hours. Already she was longing for the opportunity to spend more time with him in intimate privacy. Her legs were weak, and she had to make a small denying movement in her seat to clamp down on the sensation pulsing inside her.

She could feel Ricardo looking at her. She turned her head and looked back at him. He knew! Somehow he knew what she was feeling. The car was an automatic, and he reached for her hand, placing it against his own body.

It wasn't the answer he wanted, but it would do—for now. If her sexual response to him was her area of vulnerability, then he would have to use that to try and break down her emotional barriers.

Ricardo was hard!

Carly tried to swallow, and for one wanton shocking moment she actually found herself wishing she were the kind of woman who felt comfortable abandoning her underwear, and that only the lightness of a thin summer skirt, instead of jeans and beneath them her thong, separated her from Ricardo's intimate touch.

'Don't,' she heard Ricardo growl thickly. 'Otherwise I'll have to stop. And the back of a car just doesn't have room for what I want to do with you right now…'

'What do you want to do?' Carly encouraged him huskily.

She felt his momentary hesitation mingling with her own shock that she could be so enticing.

'I want to spread you out in front of me, your body naked and eager…just like it was that first time. I want to start at your toes, touching every inch of you, tasting every inch of you. I want to bring you to orgasm with my hand and my mouth, and watch you take your pleasure from me…'

Carly let out a soft beseeching moan. 'Stop it,' she begged. 'I can't—'

'Wait?' he demanded softly. 'Do you think it's any different for me?'

Emotionless sex! Ricardo knew perfectly well that he was brooding too much and too betrayingly over Carly's attitude. She had no idea just what emotionless sex actually was, he told himself fiercely. She had already admitted to him that she was simply trying to protect herself from being hurt, as she had been hurt as a child. And because of that she was refusing to admit that her emotions were as dangerously involved with him as his were with her. After all, she had given herself to him totally and completely as his, and he had claimed her in exactly that same way.

The figures he had been working on for making a bid for Prêt a Party were in front of him on the table of the small café where they had stopped for drink. He glanced uncaringly at them whilst he waited for Carly to return from the lavatory. He no longer cared how profitable it was, or indeed whether or not he acquired it. In fact the only acquisition he was really interested in right now was the total and exclusive right to Carly herself—preferably by way of an unbreakable and permanent legally binding document.

Where was she? His muscles tensed, and then started to relax as he saw her hurrying towards him. Two men at another table were also looking at her, and immediately he wanted to get up, lay claim to her.

'We need to stop at a chemist,' he told her as he signalled for their bill. When she looked at him in concern, he explained succinctly, 'Condoms.'

'Oh!' Carly could feel her face going pink.

'Not that I think there's any risk to either of us from a health issue point of view, but I assume you aren't protected from pregnancy?'

'Yes. I mean, no. I mean, no—I'm not protected,' Carly confirmed guiltily. How could she have overlooked something as basic and important as that?

The château owned by a famous rock star and his stunningly attractive American wife was in the Loire valley, home to some of France's famous wine-growing districts. Carly had seen photographs of the château in a magazine article about the star and his family, and she knew that his well-born wife had scoured Europe's antique dealers and employed the very best craftsmen in order to restore the building and turn it into a modern home. A mirrored ballroom similar to that at Versailles was the showpiece of the restoration work, along with the gardens.

This event was by far the largest of the three they had attended. Just about everyone who was anyone had been invited. Five hundred celebrity guests in all, mainly from the world of rock music, films, the upper classes and fashion.

In addition to a six-course dinner, the menu for which

had been organised by one of the world's leading chefs, and the regulation post-dinner dancing, the rock star's wife had chosen to have magicians moving amongst the tables, performing a variety of tricks. Cream, gold and black were the colours she had chosen, insisting that the flowers used for table decoration must not have any scent as she wanted to have the huge marquee scented only by the special candles she had ordered in her favourite room fragrance.

The marquee itself was to be black, ornamented with cream and gold, the dining chairs were cream with black rope ties, and the floor a dazzling gold that looked like crushed tissue paper beneath glass.

The house Ricardo had rented was in a small picturesque town a few kilometres away from the château on the bank of the River Loire, a tall, narrow honey-coloured stone building wedged in amongst its fellows on a dim, narrow, winding cobbled street, with its own private courtyard at the rear and a balcony on the second floor which overlooked the Loire itself.

It came complete with Madame Bouton, who was waiting to introduce herself and the house to them, explaining that she would come every morning to clean, and that she was willing to buy them whatever food they might require.

'What's that look for?' Ricardo demanded as soon as Madame had gone.

'I'm just so hungry for you,' Carly told him simply.

A sensation like a giant fist striking his chest hit him with a combination of unfamiliar emotions spiked with warnings. And then he looked into her eyes, at her mouth...

They didn't make it out of the kitchen. They didn't even make it out of their clothes. The sex was hot and immediate. Ricardo's hands cupped the bare cheeks of her bottom as he lifted her onto the table, and Carly wrapped her legs tightly round him.

She had been waiting for this and for him all day— thinking, fantasising about him, longing for him—and just the sensation of his mouth against her naked breast as he pushed aside her clothes took her to such a pitch of excitement that she thought she might actually orgasm there and then.

But, as she quickly discovered, she had more things to learn from Ricardo about the pleasure of sex. A lot more!

When he had delayed both their climaxes to the point where Carly was ready to scream with frustration, he finally complied with her urgent demands, and the intensity of orgasm that followed left her lying limply against him whilst her body shook with tremors of sensual aftershock.

Wearing her cropped jeans, a tee shirt, and a hat to protect her head from the heat of the sun, Carly stood listening to their clients as the three of them discussed the event.

'I really like the interior of the marquee, but I'm not sure now about the flowers. I think I want to change them,' Angelina Forrester informed her. 'I love the drama of having black. Perhaps if we changed things so that the tablecloths are just barely cream and the flowers black...you know, very heavy and oriental-looking. Sort of passionate and dangerous!'

Carly's heart began to sink as she recalled the trouble and the expense they had gone to in order to comply with Angelina's initial demand for scent-free blooms.

'Bloody hell, Angelina, does it matter what colour the bloody flowers are?'

The Famous Rock Star looked and sounded angrily impatient, and Carly could see the pink tinge of temper creeping up his wife's perfect complexion.

'Perhaps if we added one or two dramatic dark flowers to the table decorations?' Carly suggested calmingly, mentally deciding that if Angelina agreed to her suggestion the extra flowers would have to be artificial—or sprayed. No way was there time to source black-petalled flowers for tomorrow night! She would need to speak to the florist as well...

'Well... I'd have to see what you mean...' Angelina hesitated.

The Famous Rock Star swore crudely. 'All this because you've changed your mind about your bloody dress!'

The pink tinge had become distinctly darker.

Discreetly Carly excused herself, explaining that she needed to speak with the hired entertainers.

Arms folded over his black-clad chest, his long chino-covered legs stretched out in front of him, Ricardo propped himself up against a nearby wall and watched her.

She had good people-managing skills, and she was able to establish a genuine rapport with those she worked with. She treated them well, and with respect, and they in turn were obviously prepared to listen to what she had to say. But he didn't want her as an employee. He wanted her as a woman. He wanted her exclusively and permanently as his woman. He had, he admitted, fallen deeply and completely in love with her.

He heard a burst of laughter from the mainly male

group surrounding her and immediately his muscles contracted on a primitive surge of male jealousy.

He was halfway towards her before Carly became aware of his presence, alerted to the fact that something was happening by the sudden silence from those around her.

She turned round and saw Ricardo striding towards her, and her heart turned over inside her chest with need, her whole body going boneless with the pleasure of just looking at him.

'I thought you might be ready for some lunch.'

'Yes, I am. I think there's a sort of workers' canteen affair set up somewhere.'

Ricardo shook his head and then took hold of her arm, deliberately drawing her away from the others.

'No. Not here. I was thinking of somewhere more…private.'

She knew he could feel the betraying leap of her pulse because his thumb was resting on her wrist.

'Yes!' she told him unsteadily. 'Yes.'

Their clothes lay abandoned on the bedroom floor—Ricardo's tee shirt and her top, his chinos and her cut-offs, the smooth plain Calvins in which he could have posed as effectively and even more erotically than any male model—or so at least Carly considered—her bra, and finally the tiny side-bow-tied silky thong he had given her only yesterday. A gift for her that he would ensure brought pleasure to them both, he had told her seductively.

They lay skin to skin, Ricardo's hands slowly shaping her whilst she lay in the luxurious sensual aftermath of their earlier urgent coupling.

'You're quiet,' Ricardo murmured.

'I'm just thinking about how perfect this is and how happy I am,' Carly admitted.

Ricardo looked at her, and then cupped her face and kissed her.

'So you're ready to accept that we do have something special, that it isn't just sex, then?' he said softly.

He reached for her hand and twined his fingers through hers, holding it—and her—safely. She had fought so hard to deny what she felt, but today, lying here in the sun with him, she knew that she couldn't deny her love any longer.

'I… Ricardo, I…I do feel emotionally connected to you.'

'"Emotionally connected"?' Ricardo queried, shaking his head as he continued tenderly, 'Is the word "love" really so very hard to say? Or are you waiting for me to say it first?'

Without waiting for her to reply he kissed her gently, saying, 'I—love—you—Carly,' spacing out the words between kisses.

There could be no greater happiness than this—no greater sense of belonging, no deeper trust or awareness of being loved, Carly decided as she let him walk into her heart.

'Ricardo, we ought to get dressed.'

'Why?'

'I'm supposed to be working,' she reminded him, trying to sound as though she meant it.

'Mmm…'

Ricardo had slid his hand into her hair and was kissing the sensitive little spot just beneath her ear. But it was too late. Her own reminder to herself that she should be working had made her uncomfortably aware that she still had not dealt with the problem of Nick forging her signature.

'What's wrong?'

'Nothing's wrong. What makes you think that there is?'

'You're anxious and tense, and you're avoiding eye contact with me,' Ricardo told her wryly. 'So much for me hoping that you'd finally let me in past the barricades.'

'No, it isn't anything to do with that,' Carly assured him.

'Then what is it to do with?'

He had caught her neatly with that one. There was no point in her trying to pretend now that she wasn't worrying about anything.

'It's… It's something that doesn't only concern *me*, Ricardo.'

'The business?' he guessed.

Carly nodded her head.

'You're a potential client, and…'

He reached for her and looked into her eyes. 'I thought we'd gone way beyond that. What we have means that our personal bond with one another comes way, way before our loyalties to anything or anyone else. Surely you know that you can trust me?'

'Yes.'

'So what's the problem?'

Hesitantly, she started to explain.

'You mean to say that he's forged your signature so that he can steal from his own wife?' he said incredulously.

'I don't know that, but it does look that way. I'm just so worried about what I should do. If I tell Lucy she's going to be so hurt, and she may not even believe me.

I've been in touch with the bank and told them that no cheques are to be allowed through the account for the time being, so at least that should stop him from drawing any more.'

'How much has he taken?'

'A lot. In fact so much that the company just won't be viable by year-end unless Lucy makes up the shortfall from her trust fund.'

'So as of now the business is a sitting duck for any lurking predator?'

'Well, yes, I suppose it is. Although I hadn't thought of it in that way,' Carly admitted. 'My concern has been for Lucy and how this is going to affect her.'

'Well, you've done as much as you can do for the moment. If I were you I'd simply put it out of your mind until we get back to London.'

Strange how that one small word 'we' could mean so very much, Carly thought, as Ricardo drew her back down into his arms.

Ricardo felt the tight coiling of his own stomach muscles as Carly's nipple responded to the slow stroke of his thumb-pad. He could already see the betraying tightening of the muscles in her belly, and the now familiar way in which that threw into relief the mound of her sex.

Carly closed her eyes and gave in to what she was feeling, hoarding the pleasure to her like a child trying to hold a rainbow. She raised her head and kissed the column of Ricardo's throat, running the tip of her tongue along it, right up to his ear, then slowly and luxuriously exploring the hard whorls of flesh.

They had already made love once, but once wasn't going to be enough. She whispered to Ricardo what she wanted, her voice blurred with pleasure and longing, her body shuddering with expectation. The moment he placed his hand on her mound she spread her legs in eager anticipation and invitation, then murmured her appreciation when Ricardo parted the still-swollen lips of her sex with his fingers and started to caress her.

'What about this?' he asked thickly, rolling her over on top of him and holding her just off his own body, his mouth at the juncture of her thighs.

Carly's heart thumped excitedly against her ribs. She had wondered…been tempted…but hadn't liked to suggest such intimacy.

But now, with him holding her arched over him, his fingers exploring her wetness and then holding her open, so that his tongue could sweep the full length of her eager arousal, she could only shudder in mindless, wanton pleasure. His tongue pressed against her clitoris, caressing it into swollen heat, whilst his fingers stroked into her, finding a new pleasure spot she hadn't known existed.

Unable to stop herself she reached for him, circling the head with her own tongue, whilst her fingers worked busily on the shaft. Daringly, the fingers of her free hand moved a little lower.

She heard him groan, his whole body stiffening, and his response increased her own arousal. She could feel him lapping fiercely at her, the intimate stroke of his fingers bringing her so quickly to orgasm that she cried out in the immediacy and intensity of it.

Her body was still tingling, still quivering intensely, when he turned her over and entered her.

Immediately her muscles fastened around him, the small shallow ripples growing into violent shuddering contractions of almost unbearable pleasure.

'I love you so much,' Carly whispered, as she lay held fast in Ricardo's arms. 'I never, ever thought I could feel like this. So loved and loving, and so very, very happy.'

CHAPTER TWELVE

A SMALL tender smile curled Carly's mouth as she let herself into the house. It was lunchtime, and with the birthday ball taking place in a few hours' time by rights she should have been at the château, just in case she was needed, but instead she had given in to Ricardo's whispered suggestion that they snatch a couple of hours alone together.

Ricardo had dropped her off outside before going to park the car, promising her that he wouldn't be very long.

Any time spent apart from him right now was far, far too long, she reflected as she put the fresh bread they had stopped off to buy on the kitchen table and then, unable to stop herself, walked into the room Ricardo was using to work in.

What was it about loving someone that caused this compulsion to share their personal space, even when they weren't in it? She had become so sensitive to everything about him that she was sure she could actually feel his body warmth in the air. Half laughing at herself for her foolishness, she paused to smooth her fingers over the chair in which he normally sat. There were some papers on the desk. She glanced absently at them, and then more hungrily as she saw his handwriting.

And then, as she realised what she was looking at, she stiffened, picking up the papers so that she could study them more closely whilst her heart thudded out an uneven, anguished death knell to her love.

Ricardo frowned as the empty silence of the house surrounded him.

Carly heard him call her name, and then come down the hallway, but she waited until he had walked into the small room before she confronted him. The papers were still in her hand, and she held on to them as she might have done a shield as she accused him bitterly, 'You lied about wanting to give Prêt a Party your business. You don't want to give us anything. You want to take us over.'

'I was considering it, yes,' Ricardo agreed levelly.

'You used me! You deliberately tricked me with all those questions you asked!' Her voice was strained and accusatory, her eyes huge in the pale shape of her face.

'The only questions I asked you were exactly the same ones I, or anyone else, would have asked if they had been intending to give Prêt a Party their business.'

'You pretended to want me…to love me… because—'

'No! Carly, no—you mustn't think that.' As he stepped towards her she moved back from him. 'Yes, I had originally planned to find out from you as much as I could about the way the business is run—that's simple defensive business practice—but—'

'You accused me of being a gold-digger. But what you are, Ricardo, is far, far worse. You used me. You let me believe that you cared about me, that you loved me, when all the time what you really wanted was the business.'

'Carly, that is not true. My potential acquisition of Prêt a Party and my love for you are two completely separate issues. Yes, originally I did think I might get an insight into any vulnerabilities the business might have through you, but I promise you that was the last thing on my mind when we became lovers. In fact because of that—because of *us*—I—'

'I don't believe you.' Carly cut him off flatly. 'I thought I could trust you. Otherwise I would never have told you what I did about Lucy and Nick. I've made it all so easy for you, haven't I? Because of my stupidity Lucy will lose the company. All the time I was letting myself believe that you were genuine, that you cared about me, what you really wanted was Prêt a Party.'

'It isn't like that. When you confided in me you were confiding in me as your lover, and I can assure you *can* trust me—'

'Trust you? Carly interrupted him furiously. 'What with? You've taken all the trust I had, Ricardo, and you've destroyed it. You knew how hard it was for me to allow myself to admit that I loved you—but you didn't care what you were doing to me, did you? Not so long as it got you what you wanted. And you wanted me vulnerable to you, didn't you? The only thing that matters to you is making your next billion, nothing else and no one else. I hate you for what you've done to me, and I hate you even more for what you're going to do to Lucy.'

'Carly, you've got it all wrong. I *did* think about acquiring Prêt a Party, but once I'd met you the only acquisition I cared about was the acquisition of your love.'

Her muscles ached from the tension inside her body, and even though she knew he was lying to her, incredibly she actually wanted to believe him. No wonder she had been so afraid of love if this was what it did to her. How could she still ache for him, knowing what she did?

'You're lying, Ricardo,' she told him. 'If you weren't

planning to go ahead with the acquisition why were the papers on your desk?

'I was considering the best way to stop you worrying about Lucy and her trust fund,' he told her quietly.

Carly gave him a mirthless smile. 'Of course. And no doubt you'd decided that the best way was for you to acquire the business. You may have taken me for a fool, Ricardo, but that doesn't mean I intend to go on being one.'

'You're getting this all wrong. I can see that right now you're too upset to listen to reason—'

'Reason? More lies, you mean! I trusted you, and you betrayed that trust!' Carly could feel the anguish of her pain leaking into her voice, betraying to him how badly he had hurt her and how much she loved him.

'Trust works both ways, Carly. I could say to you that I trusted *you*, to have faith in me and my love for you. Those papers were on my desk because I was trying to come up with a way of helping Lucy without benefiting that wretched husband of hers, and the reason I was doing that was because of you. Because I love you, and I knew how upset and worried you were.'

Carly stared at him in disbelief.

'You can't really expect me to believe that,' she told him contemptuously.

'Why not? It's the truth. And if you loved me you would trust me and accept it as such.'

Tears were burning the backs of her eyes and her throat had gone tight with pain. This was the worst kind of emotional blackmail and cold-blooded cynicism, and she wasn't going to fall for it a second time.

'Then obviously I don't love you,' she told him, too brightly. 'Because I don't trust you and I don't accept it. Why should any woman accept anything a man tells

her? Look at the way Nick is cheating Lucy. It's over,
Ricardo, and it would have been better for me if it had
never started in the first place.'

Carly stared bleakly into the mirror. She hated the fact
that the only suitable outfit she had to wear for the party
was a dress that came from Barneys, which Ricardo had
paid for. Well, after tonight he could keep it—and everything else as well.

Including her heart?

She was perilously close to losing control, she
warned herself, and no way could she afford to do that.
She still had a job to do, after all.

It had been a very long day. Fortunately she had finally managed to get Angelina's approval for the flowers, even if the florist had initially been furious at the
change of plan.

Guests who had arrived early and were staying lo-
cally had started to appear at the château, wanting to
look at the marquee and demanding to see the seating
plan.

Privately Carly felt that Angelina, or one at least one
of her PAs, should have been on hand to deal with them,
but it seemed that several other members of the Famous
Rock Star's original band had already arrived, with their
entourages, and this had led to an impromptu pre-party
party taking place.

'I bet it's all sex, drugs and rock and roll up there,'
one of the entertainers had said to Carly dryly, nodding
his head in the direction of the château.

Discreetly, Carly had not made any response. But she
did know that some seriously businesslike heavies had
been hired by the celeb magazine with exclusive rights
to reporting the event to protect the guests and the event

from any unwanted intrusion by rival members of the press.

Outwardly she was conducting herself professionally and calmly; inwardly she was in emotional turmoil.

Ricardo had lied to her and deceived her, used her, and yet unbelievably, despite all that, and despite what she knew she had to do for the sake of her own self-respect, she still ached for him. Given the choice, if she could have turned back time and not seen those damning papers she knew she would have chosen to do so. How could she still love him? She didn't know how she could; she just knew that she did.

She had removed her things to a spare bedroom, and would have moved out of the house itself if it had been practical to do so. As it was, she was going to have to travel to the château with Ricardo, because it had proved impossible to book a taxi. She didn't know how she was going to endure it, but somehow she must.

And she hadn't even thought properly yet about what she was going to say to Lucy.

Ricardo was waiting for Carly to come downstairs. Did she have any idea how he felt about what she had said to him? Did she really think all the vulnerability and pain was on her side? It tore him apart to think that he had hurt her in any kind of way, and he cursed the fact that he had left those papers on his desk. He also cursed the fact that she had stubbornly refused to accept his explanation.

He heard a door open upstairs and watched as Carly came down the stairs towards him. She looked so beautiful that the sight of her threatened to close his throat. Carly's face was pale and set, and she looked very much as though she had been crying. He wanted to go to her, take her in his arms and never let her go, but he knew if he did she would reject him.

The guests had finished eating, and the magicians had cleverly kept them entertained whilst the tables were cleared. Any minute now the dancing would start.

Carly's head ached, and she longed for the evening to be over. She couldn't bear to look at Ricardo. They were seated at a small table tucked away next to the entrance used by the waiting staff. She would not be able to dance, of course; she wasn't here as a guest. Not that she wanted to risk dancing with Ricardo—not in her present vulnerable state.

Her feelings were just the last dying throes of her love for him, she tried to reassure herself. She was only feeling like this because she knew that after tonight she would never see him again. She was going to miss having sex with him, that was all.

She got up and told Ricardo stiffly, 'I'd better go and check that the bar staff have everything they need.'

He inclined his head in acknowledgement, but didn't make any response. She delayed going back for as long as she could, hoping that when she returned to the table Ricardo might have gone, and yet as she approached the first thing she did was look anxiously for his familiar dark head, as though she dreaded him not being there rather than the opposite. How was she going to get through the rest of her life without him, lying alone in her bed at night longing for him?

'The fireworks are about to start,' Ricardo warned her before she could sit down.

As a special finale to the evening a firework display had been choreographed and timed to go with music from the Famous Rock Star's biggest hit, and to judge from the enthusiastic reception the display received from the assembled guests it had been well worth the time spent on its organisation.

Carly, though, watched the display through a haze of tears, standing stiffly at Ricardo's side, aching to reach out and touch him, but refusing to allow herself to do so.

Despite what he had done she still loved him, and because of that she was hurting herself just as much as he had hurt her.

It was almost four o'clock in the morning before she was finally able to leave. She wasn't returning to the house she had shared with Ricardo though; she had arranged with one of their suppliers to return direct with them to Paris, and from there she intended to fly home. She had her passport with her, and her clothes—her *own* clothes, paid for with her *own* money—were already stowed in the supplier's four-wheel drive.

A cowardly way to leave, perhaps, but she didn't trust herself to spend another night with him. She had some pride left still, she told herself fiercely, even if he had taken everything else from her.

CHAPTER THIRTEEN

SHE had been back in London for three days now, and still hadn't been able to persuade herself to go into the office. Officially at least, so far as Lucy was concerned, she was taking a few days' leave. The reality was that she had felt too sick with loss and misery to do anything other than retreat into herself and stay in her bedroom. Fortunately Jules was away, so she had the flat to herself, but today she had to go out—because today she had an appointment to see Marcus.

No matter how much she was suffering because of Ricardo's deceit and betrayal, she reminded herself that she still owed a duty to Lucy, both as a friend and an employee, and so she had screwed up her courage and got in touch with Marcus to tell him she had some concerns about the financial affairs of the business that she did not at this stage want to discuss with Lucy. Fortunately she'd had his e-mail address, and virtually immediately he had e-mailed her back to ask her to go and see him.

The first thing she noticed when she abandoned the comfort of her 'at home' joggers and top was how loosely her jeans fitted her. It was true that she had not felt much like eating, but the sight of her pale, drawn face and grief-shadowed eyes when she looked at herself in the mirror told her that it wasn't just lack of food that was responsible for her altered appearance. But there was nothing she could take to alleviate the devastating effect of lack of Ricardo, was there? At least only she knew how humiliatingly she longed for him, despite what he had done.

Love knew no sense of moral outrage, as she had now discovered. And, equally, once it had been given life it could not be easily destroyed. She had tried focusing on all the reasons she should not love Ricardo, but rebelliously her thoughts had lingered longingly instead on the happiness she had felt before she had discovered the truth. It might have been a false happiness, but her heart would not let go of it. Her heart longed and yearned to be back in that place of happiness, just as her body yearned to be back in Ricardo's embrace.

She took a taxi to the address Marcus had given her, and was surprised to discover that she had been set down not outside an office building, but outside an elegant house just off one of London's private garden squares.

Even more surprisingly it was Marcus himself who opened the door for her and showed her in to the comfort of a book-lined library-cum-study.

'You must think it rather odd that I've got in touch with you privately,' Carly began awkwardly, having refused his offer of a cup of coffee. She was so on edge that for once she did not feel the need for her regular caffeine fix.

'Not at all,' Marcus reassured her. 'In fact…' He paused, and then looked thoughtfully at her.

'I think I have a fair idea of why you want to see me, Carly.'

'You do?'

'Ricardo has been in touch with me. He told me that you would probably wish to talk to me.'

Carly could feel her face burning with the heat of her emotions.

She couldn't understand why Ricardo should have been in touch with Marcus, but just hearing Marcus say his name made her long for him so much she could hardly think, never mind speak. But of course she had to. She took a deep breath to steady herself, and began.

'Marcus, Ricardo is planning to acquire Prêt a Party, and I'm afraid I may have made it easier for him to get the business at a lower price. You see—'

'Carly, Ricardo has no intention of acquiring the business. In fact, when he telephoned me he made it plain that whilst he had at one stage contemplated doing so, his relationship with you had caused him to change his mind. He also said that you were concerned about Nick's role within the business, specifically when it came to the financial side of things, and that it might be a good idea for me, as Lucy's trustee, to look into it.'

Carly could hardly take in what he was saying.

'But that's not true,' she protested. 'He—'

'I can assure you that it is true. In fact, Ricardo also told me that, because of your concern for Lucy and the business, he wondered if there might be some way that, between us he and I could put together a discreet rescue package, potentially with him using the services of Prêt a Party in connection with his business whilst I deal with the side of things relating to Lucy's trust fund. We agreed that we would both give some thought to our options before making a final decision.

'At that time I rather gained the impression that you and he...' Marcus paused as Carly made a small shocked sound of distress, and then continued, 'However, when he called in to tell me that you were likely to want to see me, he made no mention of your relationship. But he did ask me to give you this.'

Carly was too busy struggling to take in everything Marcus had told her to do anything more than glance vaguely at the small, neatly wrapped box Marcus had handed to her. There was one question she had to ask.

'When…when exactly did Ricardo first telephone you?'

Marcus was frowning.

'Let me have a look in my diary.'

He opened a large leather-bound desk diary and flicked through it.

'Yes, here it is…'

Ricardo had spoken to Marcus *before* she had seen the papers on his desk. He had told Marcus then about her concern and his own decision not to go ahead with any acquisition because of his relationship with her. And she had accused him of lying to her, betraying her.

She was in the taxi Marcus had insisted on calling for her before she remembered the parcel he had given her. Shakily, she took it from her bag and opened it. Inside it was a cardboard box, and inside that was her Cartier watch.

Carly tried to focus on it through the tears blurring her vision, and then realised that beneath it was a note from Ricardo which read; 'You left before I could return this to you.'

Nothing else. Just that. No words of love. But on the card was a handwritten address in London and a telephone number.

Initially he had misjudged her, but that had not stopped her loving him. Then she had misjudged him. Was his love for her strong enough to withstand that?

There was only one way she could find out.

Carly rapped on the glass panel separating her from

the taxi driver. When he pulled it open, she told him
she had changed her mind and gave him the address on
Ricardo's note.

She had paid off the taxi and now she was standing
uncertainly in front of the imposing Georgian terraced
house, its gold-tipped black railings glinting in the sunshine, and trying to remember the words she had re-
hearsed in the taxi on her way here. Words that would
tell him how much she loved him, how much she
wished she had listened to him and trusted him.

Would he allow her to say them?

Trying not to give way to the mixture of anxiety,
dread, and longing leavened with hope that was gripping her body, Carly walked up the stone steps to the
imposing black gloss-painted door, and rang the bell.

Seconds ticked by with no response. The street was
empty. Like the house? Had she let her own feelings
allow her to put an interpretation on Ricardo's note he
had never intended? Should she ring the bell again? It
was a huge house and maybe no one had heard it the
first time? Or maybe no one was there to hear it, she
told herself. But she pressed the bell a second time and
waited, whilst her heart thumped and the hope drained
from her.

There was no point in her ringing a third time.

Carly walked back down the steps, oblivious to the
fact that the reason she was struggling to see properly
was because she was crying, oblivious too to the taxi
turning into the street—until it screeched to a halt only
feet away from her, causing her to freeze with shock.

'Carly!'

Her shock turned to disbelief as the passenger door

opened and Ricardo got out, immediately striding towards her.

The taxi driver was reversing and turning round, but Carly didn't notice. She was in Ricardo's arms and he was kissing her with all the passionate hunger and love she had been longing for since she had left him.

'Come on. Let's go inside,' he told her huskily, keeping his arm round her as he guided her back up the stone steps.

'Ricardo, I'm so sorry I refused to believe you. I—'

'Shush,' he told her tenderly as he unlocked the door and ushered her into the hallway.

Motes of dust danced in the sunlight coming through the fanlight, and an impressive staircase curled upwards from the black and white tiled floor. But Carly was oblivious to the elegance of her surroundings, feasting her gaze instead on Ricardo's face.

How could she ever have thought she could live without him?

'You bought my watch back for me,' she whispered emotionally. 'And you told Marcus you didn't want to acquire the business because of me.'

'I knew you would worry about Lucy if I did, and your happiness and peace of mind are far more important to me than any business acquisition. The reason those papers you found were on the desk was because I'd seen how upset you were about Nick and the cheques, and I know Marcus vaguely, and so I'd decided that maybe it was worth making contact with him, to see if between us we couldn't do something that would set your mind at rest. I reasoned that since he was Lucy's trustee he would want to protect her, just as I wanted to protect you.'

'And then I accused you of trying to use me. I'm surprised you even want to see me again.'

'Well, you shouldn't be. Real love, true love, the kind of love I feel for you and you feel for me, is far stronger than pride—as you have proved by coming here to find me. Now, did Marcus tell you that I'm going to give Prêt a Party some business?'

'What?' said Carly blankly. 'Well, yes…'

'I've got several events in mind I can use them for, but the first and most important of them all is going to be our wedding.'

Carly looked up at him. 'You want us to get married?'

Ricardo nodded his head.

'I want us to get married; I want you to be my wife; I want you to be the mother of my children. You are my soulmate, Carly, and my life is of no value to me without you in it, at my side… But this is not the way or the place in which I had intended to propose to you.'

'It isn't?'

'No. I wanted something far more romantic—something that would make up for all the unhappiness life has brought you and show you how much I love you. A room filled with roses, perhaps, or—'

Carly reached up and placed her finger against his lips.

'I don't need or want that, Ricardo. All I want is you, and your heart filled with love for me.'

'Always,' he told her softly, before bending his head to kiss her.

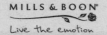